WEST OF LARAMIE

**Center Point
Large Print**

**This Large Print Book carries the
Seal of Approval of N.A.V.H.**

WEST OF LARAMIE

Les Savage, Jr.

CENTER POINT PUBLISHING
THORNDIKE, MAINE

This Center Point Large Print edition
is published in the year 2007 by arrangement with
Golden West Literary Agency.

Copyright © 2003 by Golden West Literary Agency.

The text of this Large Print edition is unabridged. In other
aspects, this book may vary from the original edition. Printed in
Thailand. Set in 16-point Times New Roman type.

ISBN-10: 1-58547-946-2
ISBN-13: 978-1-58547-946-7

Library of Congress Cataloging-in-Publication Data

Savage, Les.
   West of Laramie / Les Savage, Jr.--Center Point large print ed.
   p. cm.
   ISBN-13: 978-1-58547-946-7 (lib. bdg. : alk. paper)
   1. Large type books. I. Title.

PS3569.A826W47 2007
813'.54--dc22

2006034645

WEST OF LARAMIE

Editor's Note

"The Six-Gun Sinner" by Les Savage, Jr., was a short novel that appeared in the magazine, *Western Novels and Short Stories* (5/50). It was subsequently reprinted for the first time in book form as one of three short novels by various authors in STORIES OF THE GOLDEN WEST: BOOK TWO (Five Star Westerns, 2001) edited by Jon Tuska. In 1953, the author decided to expand this story into a book-length novel, but he ran into editorial problems about the way the manuscript ended. Of course, many of the events and what happens to the characters are dramatically different from what is to be found in "The Six-Gun Sinner", but such changes are certainly an author's prerogative. Those wishing to compare the two versions of this story can seek out the short novel, but the novel as written by Les Savage, Jr., is certainly able to stand by itself as a separate and valid work of fiction.

CHAPTER ONE

Scott Walker pushed into the Laramie Land Office, stamping Wyoming mud off his boots and slamming the door shut against the blast of wind-driven rain. The clerk behind the makeshift counter raised a sallow face, blinking owlishly.

"Damn," he said. "A night like this is enough to bring back the dead."

Scott felt his back jam tightly against the door. Then he realized it had been nothing but a casual comment. He had never seen this man before.

Smiling a little ruefully, he said: "How right you are."

The clerk looked blank. "What?"

"Nothing."

Scott moved to the counter. He was tall, twenty-five, running to lean, flat muscles and a broad chest. His face was all angles—sharp brow, sharp cheek bones, lips curled for whistling and laughing. He took off his hat, beating water off of it against his leg.

"I understand Yankee Walker has taken out a claim around here," he said.

The clerk stiffened. "Walker?"

Scott frowned. "What's the matter?"

"Nothin'." The clerk's laugh was like the rustle of dry leaves. "Nothin' at all." He straightened some papers on the counter, moved across the room toward a window. A green eyeshade cast its half-moon

9

shadow over a face like a skull. He looked more like a faro dealer than a government man.

"The Land Office at Cheyenne didn't have any record," Scott said. "But I know Yankee homesteaded somewhere near the end of track. He couldn't have gone much farther than this."

"Yeah," the clerk said. He pulled down the window shade. "I'll get my maps."

Scott walked to the potbellied stove, glowing cherry-red by a sidewall. Warming wet hands over it, he was thinking about his father now, and about his brothers. How would they take it? And mostly about Jade. How would she take it, after three years of thinking him dead?

The clerk was rummaging through a pile of ledgers and plats on a desk. He brought some of them to the counter.

"Now," he said. "Homestead or town site?"

Scott glanced sharply at him, then walked impatiently back to the counter. "I guess you didn't get it straight. I'm not here to stake any land. I'm looking for my father, Yankee Walker. . . ."

The door was thrust open behind him, admitting a rough burst of storm sound. Two men came in and closed it. One of them was tall and lanky, wearing a sodden buffalo coat over greasy buckskins soaked with rain till they looked black. He had gaunt, wolfish features with milk-pale eyes and long yellow hair bleached white by the sun. The other was short and thick as a beer keg, with a blank, open Irish face and blue-black curly hair. Water dripped from the brim of his pearl-gray hat and a gaudy bed-of-flowers waist-coat peeped between the edges of his soggy Mackinaw.

"Is this Walker?" he asked the clerk.

"One of 'em," the clerk muttered.

"Why don't you come with us?" the Irishman said. "Bannack wants to see you."

Scott remembered the clerk pulling the window shade. A premonition ran like a chilly wind through him. "What is this?" he said. "I don't know you."

"You're Walker, ain't you?"

"Scott Walker. I'm here looking for my father."

"Maybe Bannack can tell you something."

"Who's Bannack?"

"Quit playing dumb," the blond man said. He had a bright-eyed nervousness about him, like an animal in a cage. "Hi Bannack wants to see you. Come easy or come hard, make your choice."

"I don't think I'll come at all," Scott said.

The blond man made a hissing sound and the tip of his elbow flipped aside his buffalo coat. Scott had a momentary glimpse of a holstered Navy Colt before the man's hand covered its butt. For four years Scott had lived in a world where it was worth a man's life to stop and question something like this. His reactions came right out of that world, carrying him in a thoughtless lunge against the blond man before he could get his gun free.

It knocked the man back against the wall so hard the

whole building shook. Scott hit him in the stomach and it doubled him over, gun still half drawn. Scott tore it from his hand and started to wheel.

He heard a grunt, and had a dim impression of the Irishman whipping the barrel of a drawn six-shooter at him. He tried to roll with the blow, but it caught him at the base of the neck. The room seemed to explode in a million pieces and he felt the blond man's gun slip from his nerveless fingers as he fell. He struck the floor heavily and lay in a deep black well of pain and helplessness, for a moment or a year, he didn't know how long.

Finally consciousness began to seep back. He rolled to one side, groaning. Vision returned in speckled flashes and he saw the blond man still doubled over against the wall, hugging his belly, his face the color of ashes. Slowly the man straightened. Fury burned in those milky eyes, making them seem even whiter. His lips pulled back from his teeth in a wolfish snarl, and he lunged at Scott, kicking savagely at his ribs. Scott was still too dazed to roll away. The pointed boot stabbed like a knife and he couldn't help crying out in pain.

"Kalispel!" the Irishman said sharply.

The blond man stopped, foot cocked to kick again. He was breathing heavily and there was a sadistic excitement in his gaunt face. "Once more, Riordan," he said. "Just once more."

"No," Riordan said. "That's enough." He waited, with his gun in his hand, till Kalispel settled back. The blond man looked down at Scott, his face twisted vindictively. Then he bent over to pick up his Navy Colt.

The Irishman said: "Now, Mister Walker, why don't we go see Hi Bannack?"

Laramie was a new town on this May night of 1868, eagerly awaiting the arrival of the westward-moving Union Pacific tracks, a town of buildings made from logs and canvas and condemned ties and discarded wagon boxes. Window light lay in yellow smears against the rain-drenched darkness and the streets were knee-deep in mud. Huddled in his creaking yellow slicker, Scott walked between Kalispel and Riordan as they waded through the mud, crossing the street from the Land Office. They passed half a dozen freight wagons stalled hub-deep. Vague figures shuttled past lighted doorways, their voices muffled by the endless pound of the spring rain.

Scott stumbled, and Riordan caught him by the elbow. They hadn't bothered taking his gun, but Riordan still had a hand on the butt of his revolver, stuck naked in his belt. The questions were there now, along with a raw and futile anger. Did it have something to do with his father? Had Yankee got mixed up in something here?

They walked down a line of log deadfalls and tarpaper shacks to a ramshackle building with a homemade sign on its front: BELLE OF THE WEST. A rush of warmth and sound beat against them as soon as Riordan opened the door. The floor of the saloon consisted of raw planks. There was no facing on the walls. The bar was forty feet of planks knocked together. The only solid thing in the whole room was the green-topped mahogany roulette table, shipped in by wagon two weeks before. The building trembled constantly to the shifting of the mob within its flimsy walls.

Most of the men here were graders, the advance guard of the railroad crews—cursing, tough, brawling, red-shirted Irishmen who spent the days fighting Indians and weather and the country, and the nights brawling and drinking and wenching in the track-end towns that mushroomed ahead of them as they moved. The noise of them was a vast compound of clinking glasses and hoarse laughter and the monotonous chant of the bored croupiers and the chattering ball in the roulette wheel.

Riordan led the way up a flimsy stairway to a balcony. Three doors opened off it. The first admitted them to an office—no carpet on the floor, a single desk of planks, an ornate leather-seated swivel chair behind it. In the chair was a man—broad, massive, his rough-hewn face spattered with freckles, topped with a shock of fire-red hair. A big black cigar was in his mouth, jewelry on his fingers, a heavy gold watch chain linked across a striped marseille waistcoat.

Riordan closed the door on the discordant noise from below. "This the one you wanted, Hi?"

Hi Bannack frowned, took the cigar from his mouth. "What the hell?" he said.

"He was at the Land Office," Riordan said. "His name's Walker."

"Scott Walker," Scott said. "Yankee Walker's son."

Bannack leaned forward, eyes wary. "Yankee's only got two sons."

"Three."

Bannack looked at Kalispel, then at Riordan. "You damn' fools," he said.

Kalispel made a disgusted sound. "How was we . . . ?"

"Shut up!" Bannack said. He leaned back in his chair, slowly, for effect. Then he began to chuckle. "Ain't this a helluva thing?" he said. "I'm sorry, son. Yankee never told me. What's the story?"

"Maybe you'd better tell yours first," Scott said.

"Sure." Bannack rose, fingering the top of a decanter. The smell of peach brandy drifted up. He poured two drinks. "I'm in the surveyor general's office here. The government's giving the railroad twenty sections for every mile of track laid. Your dad preëmpted one of those sections before the survey was made. It's sort of a mess, but the railroad's willing to compromise. I can't have Yankee filing till he comes in here and lets us straighten it out."

Scott rubbed the back of his head. "You straighten rough."

Bannack glanced at Kalispel. "Did you do that again?"

"Like a mad dog," Riordan said.

"Get out!" Bannack said.

"Damn it," Kalispel said, "he hit me. . . ."

"Get out!"

Kalispel hung a moment on his toes, face twisted, almost sneering. Then he wheeled, with a nervous viciousness, and stalked out, slamming the door.

"I want to apologize," Bannack said. "In a rough town like this you don't have a very good choice of men."

Some of Scott's anger faded, but the pain still throbbed at the back of his neck and it wouldn't let suspicion die. He had seen enough rough towns. This wasn't that simple. But Bannack knew his father, and he decided to play along. The man handed him a drink.

"Yankee know you're coming?" Bannack asked.

Scott squinted his eyes shut and let the brandy burn out the sickness in his stomach. "They think I'm dead."

Surprise lifted Bannack's bushy red brows. "How's that?"

"The war split us up. I was wounded down South. Some mix-up in names and I was posted as killed in action. Time things got straightened up, my folks had already been burned out by Quantrill and had left Missouri."

Bannack's eyes narrowed and turned blank. "Quantrill," he said thoughtfully. "Yankee never told me that."

"Is there a girl with them?" Scott asked.

"Jade? Sure." Bannack chuckled. "Yankee's in for a big surprise." He glanced at the window, shimmering

16

with rain. "Why don't you stay here tonight? I got a spare room. We could ride out to Cheyenne Parks together tomorrow."

"I'd like to go tonight."

"Helluva storm."

"Nothing new. This Cheyenne Parks. How do I get there?"

Bannack tilted his massive head quizzically. "I guess I know how you feel. The Parks ain't hard to find. Follow the main road west out of town. About five miles you come to a fork. Right one, about a mile, and you'll be on Yankee's homestead. You'll see the lights from the road." He rose, smiling broadly, and extended his hand. "Tell Yankee to see me before he goes to that Land Office."

"I will," Scott said. He took the hand. It was a firm, manly grip, meant to allay all his suspicions. It didn't.

Downstairs, Scott moved through the dense pack of graders, smelling of wet wool and whiskey. He looked for an ash-blond head in the crowd. He saw an immense half-breed at the faro lay-out, looking at him. He reached the front door before he found Kalispel. The blond man was at the bar, drinking. There was an ornate back-bar mirror, and Scott could see Kalispel's eyes in it. Watching him.

He pushed out the door, snapping his slicker closed and pulling his hat brim down against the lash of rain. He walked up the street toward the Land Office. He passed two buildings, and then stopped by the mouth of an alley, looking back at the Belle of the West. After a moment the door opened, throwing out a blurred path of light. Kalispel came out, closing the door behind him. He wiped rain from his eyes, peering up the street.

Scott stepped back into the alley. He had seen Kalispel's kind before, the viciousness, the wild animal nervousness that would never let them relax. There was a mark to them like a brand burned on their faces, and at the end they came to this. Something twisted in their minds, something morbid that fed on viciousness, that goaded them, nagged them, prodded them, something fulfilled only by that climax, that moment of savage violence that made them perverted gods, so that they waited for it all their lives, wire-tight, hair-trigger, hating it, fearing it, sick with anticipation of it, yet needing it like dope to nourish their twisted egos. There was only one way to meet them. Reason was useless. It had to be the heel, hard, unrelenting, as vicious as they were.

Scott opened his slicker and pulled his gun. It was the Navy .36 he'd used in the war—Shiloh, Missionary Ridge, Sherman's Georgia Campaign.

The man crossed the mouth of the alley like a shadow and Scott said: "Kalispel."

With a grunt of complete surprise Kalispel stopped, elbowing aside his buffalo coat as he wheeled.

Scott was already stepping out of the alley.

"Don't."

The man saw the gun in his hand and stopped. They

stood a foot from each other, stiff as strange dogs with their hackles up. Scott reached out and got the butt of Kalispel's gun. He pulled it free and tossed it as far out into the mud as he could. Kalispel turned dead white and began to tremble visibly.

"Go back to the saloon and quit following me," Scott said. "If I see you again tonight, I'm going to take my gun and beat the living hell out of you."

For just a moment he saw fear shine in the milky eyes. A flutter of muscle ran down Kalispel's cheek and tugged at his lips. He seemed about to speak. Finally, with no more than a soft womanish sound, he turned, still trembling with fury, and started back toward the saloon.

Scott felt a little sick. Why in hell was there so much animal still left in men? He turned to cross the street. His attention had been so taken up with Kalispel that he'd failed to hear the buckboard coming up the street. The team seemed to leap out of the night at him, straining and heaving to haul the wagon through the mire. Head down against the rain, he rammed into the nigh horse.

The animal was as surprised as Scott. It emitted a frantic whinny and reared up. A front leg knocked Scott backward, and he sat down in the mud.

He could barely see the driver, standing in the seat and fighting to control the horse. But the other animal was panicked, too, and it began rearing and squealing. Their struggle cramped the tongue and finally uptilted the buckboard.

Scott saw the driver pitched out, falling face first into the mud, half buried by the barrels and boxes and sacks that spilled out of the wagon bed. The horses were thrashing madly in the harness, trying to drag the overturned rig with them down the street, but the mud mired them down. Scott got to his feet and plunged through the muck to the animals. He caught a bit and pulled the horse down. Then he flailed an arm for the other one and finally snared a rein. He held them down, quieting them with his voice. When they had settled down, he left them fiddling by the upturned wagon and waded back through the mud toward the driver. He saw the struggling form beneath a stoved-in barrel of dried apples and a hundred pound sack of flour. He tugged the sack off and clutched one of the waving arms.

"Let go, you shan muck!" The arm struck him impatiently across the chest. "I can get up myself. Buttin' through the streets like some damn' mick with a snoot full. Drunk as a grader, not enough sense t'stay in outta the rain, dumpin' your own damn' breakfast all over the terr'tory . . . !"

Scott drew back before the pummeling fists and the shrill diatribe. It was a woman's voice, and a woman's figure that finally gained its feet in the heap of sacks and barrels already sinking into the ooze. Darkness gave him but a hint of her appearance. A yellow slicker covered her body. Her hat had come off. Diffused window light from a nearby building burned against the mass of red hair that had tumbled about her face. She was still shouting at him in a rage, a string of invective that would have honored the most profane grader of the U.P. Scott held up his hands, laughing helplessly.

"Hold on, lady, I didn't see you."

"Hold on, is it? When Sean Quinn's whole crew'll have to go without breakfast for a week jist because you had to fill your snoot at the Belle o' the West. . . ."

"Nobody's filled his snoot. If you'd sound your horn this loud at the right time, you wouldn't. . . ."

"Sound my horn, is it? I'll sound my horn. I'll have every rail layer from here to Cheyenne seein' jist what you did with their dried-apple pie!"

He grinned ruefully. "Look. I'm sorry. I apologize. Let me help you get it back in the wagon."

He bent to drag a sack from the muck, but it had split open and flour spilled into the mud. It brought a fresh rush of outraged shouting from the girl.

"Take y'r hands off!" She snatched her whip out of the mud and lashed it at him in a rage. "Ain't you done enough damage already? Git outta me sight. Git outta this town before I lose me temper and show you what a real brannigan is!"

The lash caught him a stinging blow across the eyes. Half blinded, he stumbled backward, throwing his hands up for protection. The noise had drawn half a dozen graders from the Belle of the West.

"Couldn't be nobody but Penny herself," one of them said. "What's the matter, Penny?"

"This mor hooligan come staggerin' outta y'r dead-

21

fall, drunk as a lord, kicks me horses, pushes over me wagon, and then has the brass to try an' dump all me flour out in the mud."

The graders drifted toward the overturned wagon. One of them stopped by Scott, where he had backed up by a building. The man stared at the overturned wagon and clapped a hand to his brow.

"Ain't that a mess now," he said.

"It was an accident," Scott said. "Now she won't even let me help."

"We'll put 'er to rights," the grader said. "You'd better get outta town while the little girl's still calm."

"Calm?"

"Aye, 'tis a good place to be away from when Penny Quinn loses her temper."

The man waded out into the street and joined the others as they righted the wagon. Scott saw Kalispel standing against a building not three feet away. The humor of the whole thing struck him then, and Scott couldn't help laughing.

"What's so funny?" Kalispel asked sullenly.

"The fact that a girl could scare me out of town," he said, "when you couldn't."

CHAPTER TWO

Scott took the main road out of town, as Bannack had
suggested. He tried to put Bannack out of his mind.
He knew he would get the truth of the matter when he
found his family, and until then there was no use con-
jecturing. Helping to make him forget it was the picture of Jade in his mind, as it had been every day and
every night since he'd left Missouri to fight a war so
long ago.

She had been a part of his life as long as he could
remember: a girl in pigtails climbing the fence that
separated their two farms and running to meet him by
a summer swimming hole, a girl with flushed cheeks.
A few years later, when they knew for the first time
what their relationship really was, both of them were
completely wordless in the face of that knowledge.
Then she was the young woman with tears on her face,
telling him good bye on that hot August morning
when he had marched away to war, a woman so close
to him and his family that it was the most natural thing
in the world for her to move in with the Walkers when
her people were killed in one of Quantrill's raids. She
had kept writing in every letter that she was only
waiting for his return. . . .

The rain had stopped by the time he sighted the soft
glow of light from deep in timber on his flank. The
night was so black he couldn't see the trees but the
pine smell was pungent all about him. He found a trail

23

that led through dripping pines to a log house. The light came through a window glassed in by a row of bottles set on the sill. Beyond the log house now he could see another bloom of light coming from the partly open door of a hip-roofed barn. He dismounted by the log house. He dropped his reins, lifted his knuckles, knocked.

The blood was so thick in his throat that it choked him, and his heart was hammering at his ribs. Yankee. Noah. Feather. Jade.

The door was opened. She stood there, silhouetted by candlelight within. The face of her—dead white in shock—was like a piquant cameo half buried in the mass of lustrous black hair, the black eyes, smoky with the fire of a thousand passions, the fragile, uptilted nose he'd spent half a lifetime teasing her about. Her lips were soft and vivid as a child's. Then there was the figure of her: the breathtaking flare of hips within the simple cotton dress, the half seen shape of the thighs. The breasts, round and high, seemed to embody all that was woman—giving and withholding, taunting, defying, daring a man all at once.

He let his breath out in a soft, broken sound and took her in his arms. She was a thing of silken softness crushed against him, and passion roared like a bonfire in his head. He pinned her against him for a time without measure, unable to get close enough, to drink in enough. He heard her sobbing against his chest, helpless as a little child before his unexpected appearance.

"Scott, what is it? Scott, please, what is it? We thought you were dead. Oh, Scott, tell me, please. . . ."

He buried both hands in her hair and pulled her head back till her face was turned up to him. Then he kissed her on the eyes and the cheeks and the neck and finally on the lips. It was like a consummation, and, when it was over, there were tears on his face, too, and he was trembling all over.

"That little nose," he said. "I'll never tease you about it again. That sweet little nose. . . ."

She was trembling, too. With the first shock gone, her cheeks were no longer white. They were hot and flushed and she was working her body against his, making little animal sounds. Her head was thrown back, her eyes glazed, her lips slack and wet. It was a need in her as great as his own, and he kissed her again.

For a moment she gave to him savagely, passionately, her soft arms locked about his neck. Then he felt her grow rigid. Her arms were no longer about his neck. Her hands were clutching him, pushing him, struggling to get free.

"Please, Scott, please. . . ."

She tore away, stumbling backward. He followed her into the room, trying to understand the expression on her face.

"Jade," he said. "It's all right. Don't you understand? I'm all right. There was a mix-up on names."

She didn't answer. She stood against the edge of the table looking at him from eyes shimmering with tears, just shaking her head back and forth. He heard someone tramping through the soggy clearing outside, and then Noah's voice, shouting before he came into view.

"Jade, you got that hot water? Diamond finally foaled. Everything's all right now. It's a colt, black as coal. Yankee says I can have him for my stud. . . ."

He broke off as he appeared in the doorway and saw Scott. His face went blank and slack as a man with a belly blow. He seemed to sway in the doorway, surprise rendering him speechless.

He was the biggest of the family, showing little of the angular Walker shape in his face or body. Six feet tall, two hundred pounds, his weight ran to thews like an ox and beef that made thick slabs across his chest and bunched up over his shoulders. He had a broad, primitive face, almost cruelly handsome, with heavy black brows and insolent black eyes.

When he had recovered from his surprise, he let out a shout that seemed to shake the house. He ran to his brother and hit him on the shoulders with both hands, almost driving him through the floor.

"Damn you, Scott, damn you, damn you. . . ."

It was all he could say. He pounded Scott again, and then hugged him and danced him around and around. They were both laughing and cursing and pounding each other in the joy of their reunion. Finally Noah let him go and ran to the door.

"Yankee!" he bawled. "Feather! Come up here! Leave that mare to her foal and come up here like your pants was on fire!" He wheeled and ran back to Scott, grabbing his arms, again pounding him on the chest, the shoulders. "I got to make sure this is real!" he shouted. "I got to know it's you, Scott!"

Noah became aware of Jade, standing with her back to the wall now. A strange expression came to his face, and he stopped his yelling and pounding all at once. He let go of Scott and backed off, breathing heavily. He pulled at his face, like a man trying to find an adequate way to express his deep emotion.

"Well," he said. He looked at Jade again, laughing shakily. "Well, did you ever think somethin' like this would happen . . . in a million years?"

There was a tramp of feet outside. Yankee and Feather came to the door, and stopped. It was the same surprise again, the same moment of helpless silence. Then Scott's father and kid brother were on him, pounding his back, grabbing his arms, laughing with tears in their eyes. After a moment Yankee pulled back. He sunk his chin self-consciously against his neck, digging furrows in the leathery flesh of his jaw. He had always been a gruff man, repressing emotion, a little ashamed of it. But even after the first display he couldn't completely hide what this meant to him. He jammed his knobby farmer's hands into the pockets of his linsey-woolsey trousers and stalked across the room, sending sidelong glances at Scott out of his hazelnut eyes. He was a tall, bony man, all elbows and knees. His hair stood up in a dead white shock, thick and coarse as a horse's roached mane. His

27

face was a thing of gaunt hollows and bony ridges with a Puritanical heritage in the burning, deep-set eyes and the stern lips.

"I never would've left Missouri," he said. "You know that, Scott. If I'd had any idea you were alive, I would've hunted the world over. But we got the notice. Straight from the War Department. You'd been killed in action."

Scott nodded. "I know. It was a mix-up in names. A whole bunch of us got it at once, in a draw. I was picked up by the Rebels and sent to Savannah. The truth didn't get back to the War Department for months."

Little muscles knotted along Yankee's bony jaw, and he jammed his hands deeper into his pockets. "The news must've come after we left Missouri. Quantrill burned us to the ground, Son. It was worth a man's life to stay in that part of the state."

Feather glanced at his father, eyes dark. "Let it be, Pa," he said. He wheeled back to Scott, circling him, unable to remain still in his excitement. Feather was the youngest of the three brothers, eighteen now, too young for fighting when the war had come. Boy-like, he was ashamed of the fragile beauty of his face and was always slicking his hair down with bacon grease to take the curl out of it. He had a slender dancer's body, every motion as skittish as a Thoroughbred. He glanced at Jade, still standing by the wall. A frown touched his face. Then he grabbed Scott's slicker, smiling again. "You got to get dry. You got to tell us all about it."

Scott saw that Yankee was looking at Jade, too. His eyes seemed to burn, deep in their sockets, and his lips were stern as a deacon's. Damn them, Scott thought affectionately. If it was that plain how much he wanted to be alone with her, why didn't they clear out?

But he didn't want them to go. He wanted them all around him, wanted to drink in the rough warmth and the kinship that had been so foreign to his life these last years. He moved to the wood stove, holding his hands over the welcome heat. He was reluctant to resurrect the war years. It was a dark corner of his life he wanted to forget as thoroughly as possible. He sketched it briefly for them. He'd lasted through all of Sherman's long march to the sea—Kennesaw Mountain, Atlanta, Nashville, Savannah—the sieges and the burning. At Cole's Farm, so close to the end, the Minié ball had found him, a bad wound, keeping him in the Savannah hospital a year after the war's end.

After that, the search. The only hint of them he could get in Missouri was from Kaufman, a neighboring farmer who had returned after Quantrill had left. Yankee had told Kaufman they were heading West, perhaps Kansas, or Nebraska. A year of scouring the two states, and then another hint in Omaha. A storekeeper from whom Yankee had bought a wagon. He thought they were headed for Montana. Scott's search up there had been fruitless and he had turned south again, checking the Land Offices, knowing Yankee's love of the land. At Cheyenne he had got his first real lead. . . .

When he finished talking, there was silence. Noah was watching him fixedly. When Scott looked at him, the man's eyes dropped to the table. Scott saw the same strange watchfulness in his father's eyes. He tried to smile.

"You still think you're looking at a ghost?"

Feather shifted uncomfortably by the stove. "Yeah," he said. "Guess that's it."

Yankee looked at Jade. There was fire and brimstone in his eyes. "You ain't told him?"

She moved her head from side to side, like someone in pain. "I . . . I didn't have a chance."

Yankee continued to look at her, as if waiting for her to speak. She closed her eyes. Yankee turned to Scott. The grooves were deep about his mouth and sweat stood in little bands on his bony brow. "I guess it's up to me," he said. "Jade's married, Scott. She's Noah's wife."

CHAPTER THREE

It was a good piece of land Yankee had chosen. There was water on it, a creek that was full to the banks now with yellow spring water, tumbling out of a notch in the ridge, rioting through the dense stands of timber that finally opened out into green-grassed parks, gurgling past the house and barn and corrals where they stood on a gentle slope overlooking the road.

Scott saw it all that next morning. He had spent a sleepless night and he had rolled out with dawn and walked to the ridge, sitting among the moss-black boulders and rolling cigarette after cigarette from the makings Noah had given him last night.

There was a sick emptiness in Scott. It was an effort to dredge up any feeling, any thought. He didn't want to dwell on the rest of last night, after Yankee had told him of the marriage. They had all known what it meant to him, yet none of them had been able to put it into words. It had been like a macabre little melodrama, with all of them going through their mechanical pretenses, the words that meant nothing, the expressions that masked emotion, the subdued torture in Jade's eyes, the defiance in Noah's.

It had come as a great shock. He had not been completely blind to the possibility of Jade's marrying. It was the logical assumption, with a girl of her beauty. But every meager hint he'd got about his family had indicated just the reverse—had convinced him that, although she believed him dead, her love for him still lived, holding her apart for a while, standing between her and any other man. The very fact that she had been with his family had substantiated that. Why hadn't he seen the obvious answer? The thought of Noah simply hadn't occurred to him—because Noah had been the reckless one drawn to the racy town girls and never showed anything but a teasing tolerance of Jade, because Noah had been such an integral part of that old pattern of life in which Jade had so obviously belonged to Scott that it was accepted as unquestion-ingly as the rising of the sun.

Scott saw the movement in the timber below the rocks, and stood up. Jade emerged from the trees. She was breathing hard from the climb and it pushed her bosom high and taut against the flimsy calico dress. Her walk imparted a free, womanly sway to her hips and morning sunlight flashed against bare white calves. Her black hair was coiled and braided and held on top of her head with a comb. Her cheeks were flushed with exertion, and she was a little girl and a woman, passion and tenderness, cruelty and sweet-ness all at once.

She stopped before him, making no effort to smile. "I thought maybe you'd be up here," she said.

"I wanted to be alone," he said.

"I won't apologize for intruding," she said. "I had to talk with you. I couldn't really say anything last night in front of them."

He tried not to feel bitter. Only a stupid fool would be bitter. "What's there to say?" he asked.

"So much," she said. She searched his face, eyes luminous. Then she shook her head and sat down on the rocks. The wind boomed up out of the timber and tore tendrils of her hair loose. She brushed them off her temple, staring at the ground. "Help me, Scott. I want to tell you . . . somehow."

"I'm sorry for how I acted last night," he said. "I guess I should have taken it better."

She looked up at him, little muscles drawn tautly

about her soft lips. "You took it very well. What else could you have done? You said the right thing."

"Made the right grimaces," he said. He smiled ruefully. "I guess it was as hard on them as it was on me."

"No," she said. "I don't believe that."

He looked directly into her eyes, and it was like the pain of a knife in him. He turned his back on her and looked off into the valley. His cigarette had burned down and he dropped it, and ground it out with a heel. Why couldn't he be honest? There had been a moment last night when he had wanted to kill Noah.

She stood up, so close to him he could feel the heat of her body, speaking in a brittle, trembling voice. "We were only married a few months ago, Scott. That's how long I waited. Even though I thought you were dead, that's how long I waited."

"I wanted to believe that," he said. "I wanted to believe it would take you a little while to get over me, even if you thought I was dead."

"Three years, Scott. Almost three years. What would you do, after that much time?"

"I don't know. I'm trying to understand."

"Noah has something of you in him. Maybe that's part of it. I was so lost, Scott . . . so lost. . . ."

He didn't want to ask it. Didn't want to say the word. Yet he couldn't hide from it any longer.

"And you love him?"

She didn't answer. The wind boomed high through the trees again. It sounded like the barrage at Atlanta.

He turned around and she was staring at him with

that torture shimmering on the surface of her wide black eyes. She began to move her head from side to side and the words sounded squeezed out of her.

"Scott . . . Scott. . . ."

"I've got to know," he said. "That's the only real answer, isn't it?" His voice sounded bitter now, despite himself. "You don't marry a man unless you love him, do you?"

She bit her lip and squinted her eyes shut. "Scott . . . I thought I did . . . I thought I did. . . ."

"And now?"

She stared at him a moment longer, completely lost. Then she put her hands to her face. The sobs came from deep within her body, causing her to shudder. She turned, her shoulders bowed, her hands still covering her face, and stumbled down the slope. The sound of her sobbing tore at him and he followed her, wanting to stop her, to help her, to tell her that he understood, that he didn't want to hurt her. She must have heard him, for she started running faster down through the trees. Before he could catch her, he heard a jingling sound, and Yankee appeared in the trees, leading a span of mules dragging a heavy sled made of whipsawed lumber.

Yankee checked the team and watched Jade stumble past him. His face, burned mahogany brown by a lifetime of weather, was set in stern lines. Scott slowed his plunging run, coming to a stop by the mules. They were sweating from the climb and the smell of them was rank.

Yankee was not a flexible man. If he had come up here to part Jade and Scott, there was no admission of it in his face.

"Have you settled it?" he asked.

"Did it look that way?"

"Don't take that tone with me," Yankee said. "This is a bad, twisted thing. I've got to know what you mean to do."

Scott ran a hand through his black hair. "I'm sorry, Pa. You must know how it hit me." He looked into his father's eyes. "Is she really in love with him?"

"Of course she is. It's a good marriage. You've got to accept it, Scott. I can understand what a surprise it was. But it's done. We all want you here. But if you stay, you've got to accept it. She's his wife now. That's the end of it."

That was Yankee. Good or bad, wrong or right, black or white, nothing in between, no gray shades, no doubts, no questions. Couldn't he see the confusion in Jade? Couldn't he see what a hopeless mess it was?

Maybe he saw some of it in Scott's face. Little crow tracks sprang up about Yankee's squinting eyes and something akin to a smile touched his lips. It was the nearest approach to an expression of sympathy he could show after such a display of emotion last night. He put a hand on Scott's shoulder. Scott could feel the crust of calluses on the palm through his shirt.

"Help me dig up some of these rocks," Yankee said. "Good, hard work will settle anything."

They walked together over the ridge and down into

35

one of the parks overlooking the Laramie road. Yankee had a crowbar and a spade over one shoulder. He jammed the bar under the first big rock they met, and they both put their weight on it, prying out the boulder, hoisting it onto the sled. It was hard work, and they were both dripping sweat by the time they got the sled loaded. Yankee drove it to the edge of the park, and they began piling rocks into a wall.

"This side's prime for alfalfa," Yankee said. "I can divert the creek in dry years. Turn the other slope to horse pasture. All this cattle coming north, there'll be a big demand for good cow ponies."

The shock of finding Jade married had driven the thought of Kalispel and Bannack from Scott's mind. Yankee's talk of the land brought it back. Scott sat on the heap of rocks, mopping his brow, and told Yankee about it. When he had finished, Yankee scowled at the ground.

"This Kalispel and Riordan must have been waiting for me. When you said you were Walker, they thought they had their man."

"You've never seen them?" Scott asked.

"Neither of them," Yankee said. "I made my deal with Bannack, some months back, before Laramie was even a town. These other two are new to me."

"What'd they want to stop you from doing in that Land Office?" Scott asked.

"Sounds like they wanted to keep me from perfecting my title," Yankee answered. Then he told Scott the story. When they had arrived the year before, there had been no Land Office nearby. So Yankee had preëmpted the land, getting a four-pole chain and running his own lines. When the Land Office had been established at Laramie, he had gone in to file for his homestead patents. He was told that the government had promised twenty sections of land to the railroad for every mile of track laid, and that Cheyenne Parks fell in one of the chosen sections. That had been a bitter blow to the Walkers, with a year of backbreaking work behind them, their house and barn built, a crop ready to harvest.

"That's where Bannack came in," Yankee said. "He's the deputy surveyor for this district. He told me this was a common occurrence. A lot of settlers who'd preëmpted before the survey were taking it to court on the basis of squatter's rights. The railroad usually won, but the litigation cost them a lot of time and money. To save the expense they're usually willing to make a deal. If the land is of no value to them, their land company would sell it for two dollars and fifty cents an acre, payable in installments."

"Sounds straight."

"I thought so, too. Bannack said the only thing of value to the railroad was the timber. They'd close the deal if I'd lease timber rights. That would only mean a few acres, and I swallowed that, too, till Bannack showed up with a ninety-nine year lease."

"That's not uncommon."

"You don't need ninety-nine years to cut the ties. And the lease was to a private contractor."

"The U.P.'s farming out a lot of their work."

"To Gaelbreth Riordan?" Yankee asked. Scott looked up sharply and Yankee nodded. "You see what I mean. A legitimate contractor doesn't go around slugging people."

The breeze boomed up out of the timber and swept the smell of sun-warmed pitch to Scott. From the somber pools of shadow under that same timber the riders appeared. Hi Bannack was in the lead, a broad and primitive shape on his potbellied livery nag. Behind him, on one flank, rode Riordan. On the other flank was Kalispel.

Scott stood up. He had left his gun at the house and he cursed himself for it. He moved to the crowbar, leaning against the rocks. There was only the sound of the grunting horses and the *creak* of saddle rigging as they climbed up the steep slope. Then Hi Bannack reached them, pulling his winded animal to a halt, grinning broadly.

" 'Morning, Yankee. Looks like you been working hard."

"I always work hard."

The edge left Bannack's humor. He looked at Scott. "How does it feel to have him back?"

"I was thankful," Yankee said.

Kalispel's horse fiddled, chirping on its cricket. Kalispel sat tall in the saddle, watching Scott with an unwinking, baleful gaze. Scott saw that his gun was back in its holster.

"Railroad'll be in Laramie in a few days," Bannack

said. "Riordan's got to start cutting ties. We brought the lease."

Adamant lines carved themselves into Yankee's stern face. "I'm not signing, Bannack."

All the humor left Bannack's face. His lips pinched tightly and his eyes turned to silver disks, glittering in the sun. He put broad hands on his saddle horn and leaned his massive weight against them.

"You know the land's not yours yet."

Yankee glanced at Kalispel. "So you plant your muscle men to keep me from perfecting my title."

"You sign the lease," Bannack said, "you can file."

"Maybe I can file anyway," Yankee said. "Maybe that's why you're so afraid I'll show up at that Land Office."

Riordan pulled his horse closer, a bland smile on his face. "You're being unnecessarily stubborn, Mister Walker. I've made a hundred deals like this, all along the right of way."

"We'll see," Yankee said. "I've written Omaha. If you've got authorization, I'll know soon enough."

Riordan glanced sharply at Bannack. "We can't wait that long. We've got to have those ties right now. Two thousand, six hundred and forty of them to every mile. We're so low on hardwood we can only use four to a rail. We're burnetizing the cottonwood and hunting high and low for red cedar. . . ."

"Shut up!" Bannack said. Riordan glanced angrily at him but Bannack did not even notice. He reined his horse hard against Yankee, forcing him back against a tree and pinning him there with the animal's flank. His voice was vicious. "You made a deal with me, Yankee, and, damn it, you're going through with it. Riordan's got the lease and you're going to sign it. . . ."

Still holding the crowbar, Scott grabbed at the horse's bit. "Stay away, Bannack!" he called. "You're hurting him."

"Stay out of this!" Bannack shouted. He yanked on the reins, keeping the horse against Yankee. "Kalispel, take care of him."

The blond man wheeled his pony and started to draw his gun. Scott let go Bannack's bit and swung the crowbar up in an arc. The cast-iron bar struck Kalispel heavily across the ribs. He let out a broken shout and pitched from the saddle.

The panicked pony charged directly into Riordan and the man had all he could do to stay on his horse. Kalispel lay doubled up on the ground, groaning in pain, his gun five feet away. Scott ran and scooped up the six-shooter, whirling toward Riordan. The Irishman had just quieted his horse, and held up both hands empty.

"Nothing for me, lad, nothing for me."

At the same time, Scott saw that Yankee had pulled Bannack off his horse. He was standing astraddle, holding the man up off the ground by his coat to hit him in the face. The blow knocked Bannack back so hard it tore his coat. He flopped away from Yankee, trying to gain his feet, but Yankee followed and caught him again. There was a glazed look to Yankee's eyes,

40

a burning fury in his face that shocked Scott. He again held Bannack up off the ground by his clothes and hit him again, and again.

Bannack's whole body jerked with each blow. He struggled to tear free but Yankee held him now with a maniacal strength, making a strangling sound every time he hit the man.

"This is my land, Bannack." Hitting him. "You bastards burned me out once." Hitting him. "Everything I had, everything I'd worked a lifetime for." Hitting him. "You won't do it again, Bannack . . . you won't."

Bannack's head rolled loosely. His face was slack and smeared with blood, and he started sliding to the ground. Yankee caught him by his red hair and pulled him up to hit him again. His teeth were bared and he snarled.

"Yankee!" shouted Scott. "Stop it! He's done!"

Yankee didn't seem to hear. He struck again, and Bannack's head jerked and flopped back and his body was a dead weight pulling on Yankee. Riordan shouted: "Stop him, son, he'll kill Hi!"

Scott ran to his father, grabbing his arm. Yankee flailed at him, trying to get free in order to hit Bannack again. Yankee's strength was frightening. Scott fought to pull him away, yelling: "Pa, stop it! Are you crazy? You'll kill him! Stop it . . . !"

Yankee stumbled backward, almost fell. He checked himself, swaying there. He made a wheezing sound, like a hurt animal. He looked at his bloody hands. He raised his eyes to Scott, shaking his head slowly from side to side. He looked at Bannack, lying on the ground. Finally he shook his head again, turned, and shambled to the rock fence. He sat down on it and put his face in his hands.

"Get 'em out of here," he said in a groaning voice. "Get 'em out."

Riordan dismounted and got a flask from his hip pocket. It took a long time to bring Bannack around. Kalispel was on his feet, walking around in a circle and holding one hand on his ribs.

Scott didn't bother answering. He got Bannack's horse and led it to the man where he sat on the ground, too dazed and sick to speak. He helped Riordan get Bannack on his feet and hoist him into the saddle. Bannack leaned over the horn, bleeding from the nose. Riordan mounted and sided Bannack to hold him in the saddle. The red-haired man straightened up, looking at Scott, then at Scott's father.

"Yankee," he said.

Yankee lifted his head up. The two men stared at each other without speaking.

Bannack coughed, and blood came from his mouth. "You'll wish to God you hadn't done this," he said.

CHAPTER FOUR

Scott watched the three riders disappear down the hill. He didn't want to look at his father again. He had seen his father's rages before. But nothing quite like this. He remembered the darkness that had come to Feather's face last night, when Yankee had started telling how Quantrill had burned them out. Could it do that to a man? A capacity for towering rage, love of the land that approached an obsession. Could it do that?

Somebody began clanging a triangle from the house, and Yankee rose. He was trembling and his face was white. "Breakfast," he said. "Let's go."

It was a dismal meal. None of them tried to talk. Aside from some split knuckles and bruises on his hands, Yankee bore no signs of the fight, and he didn't volunteer any word of it to the others. Jade ate with her face turned down, avoiding Scott's eyes. She finished only half her meal, and then rose and busied herself with the dishes. Scott had little appetite, either. Finally he pushed back his chair and went outside to roll a cigarette. There was a gilded haze beneath the pines now and the smell of wood smoke made the air pungent. Why couldn't a man have this peace? Why was something always tearing at him?

Noah came out and stopped two feet away, studying Scott dourly. The strong, bright light accented the primitive sculpturing of his face. There had always been a sullen streak in Noah. When it came to the surface, he reminded Scott of a little boy pouting.

"I think we should talk, Scott."

Scott took a deep drag on the cigarette. "It's a helluva thing to find words for, Noah."

"You haven't got no right to blame us."

"And you haven't got no right to feel guilty, Noah. I'd have done the same thing in your place."

Noah seemed to relax a little. "You going to stay?"

Scott shook his head. "I don't know."

"It ain't that we don't want you. But you got to understand one thing."

"What's that?"

Noah took a step closer. His voice was husky.

"She's mine, Scott. You ain't got no more claim on her. She's my woman."

Scott dropped the cigarette and ground it under his heel, trying to hold back the antagonism. He wanted to feel kinship, warmth, understanding, the love of brother for brother. He wanted to keep all this straight and not let it get twisted because there was nothing really that should make them antagonists. They were both caught in this, equally as helpless, equally as blameless. He was sure Noah was reacting from sincere emotions. He would have felt the same way Noah felt now, unsure, on the defensive, suspicious. He wanted to understand all this in his brother.

Yet there had always been a barrier between them that he had never been quite able to surmount, and he couldn't help feeling the antagonism for Noah, taking

44

it that way, black and white, right and wrong, nothing in between: Jade was his, no questions, no doubts.

"Don't you think that's something for Jade to decide?" he asked.

"She decided it when she married me." The color dyed Noah's cheeks deeper, and there was a little knot of muscle at the top of his mouth. "You ain't got no right to come here and start twisting things up."

"Noah," Scott said, "if I thought Jade loved you, finally and completely, if I thought that she wanted it this way from now on, even knowing I was alive, I'd leave right now."

Noah was inches away, his fists closed, his breath hot against Scott's face. "She does, Scott."

Scott knew it was stupid to go on, but he couldn't stop. "You keep speaking for her," he said. "Are you afraid to let her speak for herself?"

Noah made an inarticulate sound. The weight of his whole body shifted. Scott's impulsive reaction made him twist and start lifting his right arm to block a blow. Before it could come, Yankee stepped from the door, wiping his mouth with the back of his hand.

"Noah!"

Noah stopped, face rigid, body lifted onto his toes. He settled back finally, with the air leaving him in a long, stertorous grunt.

"We're riding into Laramie," Yankee said. "I'm going to see about filing on the land."

Yankee's boots scratched angrily against the ground. Noah looked at him, and then bowed his head and turned to tramp toward the barn. Scott watched him go. He had forgotten how subservient Noah was with Yankee. Able to whip any man in town, he was a cowed dog with his father. Scott had forgotten how subservient they all had been.

He glanced at Yankee, almost in guilt, and turned to go inside. Jade stood at the wooden sink, her back to Scott. Feather sat at the table, looking emptily at his greasy plate. Scott went into the second room and took his holstered gun out of his bunk, buckling it on. When he came out again, Jade's back was still toward him. He stopped, looking at her. She did not turn.

Feather rose and got his gun and accompanied Scott out.

"Why does it have to be this way?" he asked miserably. "Having you back should be the best thing that ever happened to us."

Scott tried to relax. He'd always had a deep affection for Feather. They had more of their mother in them than Noah, and it gave them a bond. He put his arm around Feather's shoulder.

"Let's not think about it, kid. I saw a lot of dirty things in the war. I wanted to forget it. I told myself that, when I got out of it, there wasn't going to be a day when I didn't laugh and sing and live like a man's supposed to, even if I had to spend my time drunk to do it."

Feather brightened. "Maybe we should stop off at the saloon."

"I think we should," Scott said. "I think that would be a helluva good idea."

Before they reached the corrals, Yankee and Noah rode out and down the trail. Feather and Scott looked in on the newborn colt for a moment. They laughed together over it, and that was a good thing, a small fragment of what Scott had looked forward to during all the long search.

"Try that pied horse for a single-foot," Feather said. They saddled up, and, when Feather had his cinch tightened, he leaned against his bay, watching Scott draw his latigo tight. Scott looked up and their eyes met. Feather shook his head, and then slapped his saddle. "Damn, it's good to have you back," he said.

Scott swung into his saddle, wondering what kind of brotherhood Feather had known with Noah, this sensitive, sunny, reaching-out boy with all his groping, inarticulate needs—and that surly, reckless, imperceptive man. Why hadn't he seen these relationships before? Why hadn't he remembered them during the years he was away?

"You got any books?" he asked.

Feather glanced at him in a puzzled way. "Ma's books were burned when Quantrill hit us."

"I remember you reading," Scott said. "When I look back, I think of you lying on the floor and reading."

"Ma was alive then," Feather said.

"Yankee work you hard?"

"No more'n usual," Feather said.

"Any girls?"

"None anywhere near."

"We'll find one," Scott said. "A nice, shy, soft one.

Man needs a little softness in his life."

Feather looked off at the timber with blank eyes. "I'd like that," he said.

Scott kicked the pied horse into its single-foot and Feather had to canter his bay to keep up. It was a fine rhythmic gait that didn't come often to any horse and it brought them up swiftly on Noah and Yankee. They settled down to a walk and all four rode in silence for a while, with a subtle tension beginning to stir through them. Scott knew what it was. He wondered if Bannack would have anybody waiting at the Land Office.

Two miles, maybe three. Then the sound of a hard-ridden horse came into view behind and the sight of Jade on an animal so rimed with lather that its original color was hardly discernible. She rode bareback, astride, and her skirt had climbed high on her gleaming legs. She began to shout while she was still at a great distance.

"The barn's on fire. Can't you see the smoke? I couldn't stop it alone. Can't you see the smoke?"

Scott's eyes lifted automatically to the sky. It was darkening above the timber, like soot staining a turquoise sea. All four men reined around and put their horses into a dead run. They passed Jade before she could turn. Yankee led off the road and straight up a slope. It was a wonder they didn't go down in the rock-strewn parks, with their headlong ride. But Yankee cut a mile of road off by his short cuts. They finally topped a ridge and saw the hollow below. Fanned by a vigorous wind, red flames shot up in a

48

hundred angry tongues from both the house and the barn, losing themselves in the billows of black smoke that hung over the whole valley like a sinister pall. Jade caught up with the men as they started down the slope; her panting, fear-ridden voice came to Scott, warped on the wind.

"I tried to let some of the horses out. I couldn't do it all in time."

Scott knew a poignant fear as he thought of that helpless, fuzzy foal. "How about the colt?"

"In the north end. I thought it would be safe there till I reached you."

Yankee swung off his horse in the compound. "Feather, Noah, all the buckets you can find. Fill 'em at the water trough. All we can do now is hope to save our stock."

Scott was with him as they rushed into the choking smoke. Horses were squealing and fighting to get out of their stalls. Scott shouted in pain as a tongue of flame licked out to scorch him. Noah and Feather ran in with buckets of water, sloshing down a heap of burning hay so Scott could get through to the foal. The animal was quivering and whimpering in panic. He had to pick it up in his arms, and staggered into the open with the half-crazed mare following him. Yankee ran out leading a pair of mules by their halters. Jade appeared in another moment, driving a bawling milch cow.

The five of them couldn't supply enough water to stop the blaze now. Feather and Noah could only follow the others with their buckets and try to wash out the blaze here and there long enough for Scott or Yankee to reach a stall.

Once in the open, there was no holding the animals. Wild with fright and the pain of their burns, they broke for the timber. All the men could do was stand, helpless and exhausted, after they had saved the stock, watching their dreams burn down to charred ashes.

There was a stunned look on Jade's smudged face. She stood beside Noah, pushing at her hair. "I couldn't stop it," she kept repeating. "I'd gone to the creek for water. I saw the house burning first when I came back. I went up there. Then I saw the barn. I couldn't stop it, Noah. I couldn't. . . ."

"All right," Noah said viciously. "So you couldn't."

Feather looked at him, eyes stricken. The wall of the barn fell in with a great crash, and embers leaped like shooting stars into the smoke. Yankee quivered as if from a blow. He stared at the barn with a terrible fury burning in his eyes. His mouth looked like a twisted scar carved into a stone face.

"I know who did this," he said. His voice was guttural, broken. "I know who did this."

Scott remembered that same look to his face, that maniacal fury in him, when he had been hitting Bannack. Yankee wheeled suddenly, jerking like a puppet on a string, and started toward the frightened saddle horses they'd left at the edge of the clearing.

"Get your horses," he said. "We're going to Laramie."

Feather came quickly to Scott's side. "We'd better stop him."

Scott glanced sharply at the boy, then they both started after Yankee. "Feather," Scott asked, "what is it? What's got into him?"

Feather shook his head. "I don't know. Ever since Quantrill burned us out, he's been bad, Scott."

"He's always had a temper."

"Not like this. You should have seen him when we lost the Missouri place. Like a crazy man, for days. Noah and I had to tie him down to keep him from going after Quantrill. It would have been suicide. I think it twisted him, Scott. You know how much the land meant to him."

They caught up with Yankee as he reached his horse, and Scott grabbed his arm. "Pa, why don't you wait till you cool down? It could have been anything. A spark from a cigarette."

"Not both buildings." Yankee tore loose, reaching for his saddle horn.

Scott caught his arm again. "What if it was Bannack? How can you prove it?"

"Damn you!"

Yankee tore loose and heaved him back so violently Scott almost fell. Then he swung into the saddle and sat there like a raging god, eyes blazing down at them. "They can't do it to me twice. I thought I'd taken all I could the first time. This is too much, Scott. They can't do it to me twice. . . ."

His voice broke, and he sounded as if he were sobbing as he wheeled the horse and headed it at a dead run toward the Laramie road. Scott looked at Feather, and he felt sick. He knew they had to follow Yankee. But for just that moment he couldn't move, for just that moment he was remembering Yankee and Bannack earlier in the day.

"What does he mean, twice? He said the same thing to Bannack before."

Feather was looking after his father. "Yankee just found out yesterday . . . in town," he said. "During the war, Bannack rode with Quantrill."

CHAPTER FIVE

On May 9, 1868, the Union Pacific tracks reached Laramie. The first train slid down the steep grade into town and with it came all the freight, human and otherwise, of the "Hell-on-Wheels". Gangs of whooping, red-shirted graders rode the first flat cars, piled high with the plows and scrapers of their trade. Behind them, clinging to flats heaped with rails and cross-ties, were the rail layers—Black Irish, Red Irish, drunk Irish, singing Irish. On the cars behind them were heterogeneous heaps of tents and portable shanties, lumber and groceries, cook stoves and crockery, tinware and kegs of whiskey; and on the final cars rode the peripatetic, parasitical population of the terminal towns, the faro dealers and card sharks and monte throwers and con men and prostitutes and saloon-keepers and peddlers and shills and gunmen for hire who followed the rails, blooming with each terminal town as they reached it, sucking it dry, deserting it for the next one as soon as the rails moved on.

They were dropping off the train before it had stopped, swarming up the muddy streets of Laramie, hooting gangs of Irishmen looking for the first saloon and fancy women eying the buildings for a place to set up shop and thimble riggers putting up their little three-legged tables before the stores and shills beginning their spiels. Into the indistinguishable babble and swarming movement of this mob rode the Walkers.

Scott and Feather and Noah had not been able to catch their father on the road. He'd had a head start and rode the horse with the most bottom. After miles of running, the three brothers had been forced to slow down to keep from killing their animals. They pulled up on the edge of the brawling crowds now, looking over the sea of bobbing heads for sight of Yankee's lathered roan.

"I don't think he'd go to the Land Office," Scott said. "But one of us had better check."

"Why bother?" Noah said. "I think Pa's right. The vigilantes are the only law in this town and they won't touch Bannack for this. If he's gonna pay, it's gotta be up to us."

"I don't give a damn about Bannack," Scott said. "Right now Yankee's all that worries me. If he starts a row all by himself, they'll cut him down. Our first job is to find him."

Noah gazed at him sullenly, then turned his horse

into the mob. Scott edged to the side of the street and started down toward the saloon. Before he reached it, he could see another rider enter from a cross street and quarter through the crowd toward the saloon. It was Jade, on a lathered black horse.

"She must have hopped the ridges," Feather said.

"I told her not to follow us," Scott said angrily.

They had saved some of the tack from the blaze and Jade had thrown a saddle on the black. She had run the life out of the animal for it was stumbling and wind-broken and bleeding from its flaring nostrils. Feather called to Jade but the noise was too loud for her to hear. A gang of drunken graders began shouting at her as she pulled in at the saloon rack and stepped off. She brushed wind-blown hair from a smudged face, looking around searchingly.

A man disengaged himself from the crowd and walked up to Jade. He was tall, blond, handsome, dressed in khaki and jackboots, a red bandanna knotted around his sun-bronzed throat. He took off his hat as he spoke to her. A smile came to her troubled face and she brushed at her hair again with a sudden feminine consciousness of how smudged and bedraggled she was.

"Who is it?" Scott asked.

"Harvey Kane," Feather said. "Surveyor for the railroad."

"He must work out of Bannack's office, then."

"I suppose so," Feather said.

As they forced their way through the last of the mob

to the rack, Scott looked around for Yankee's lathered animal. With only half his mind on the question, he asked: "Does Bannack really operate out of a saloon?"

"I think he owns a piece of it," Feather said. "The surveyors always come ahead of the rails. It gives him a chance to get his fingers in the best pies before anybody else."

Jade was talking intently with Kane and he was nodding soberly, politely. But Scott could see his eyes on the curves of her fine body beneath the flimsy, soot-blackened dress, could see the flush creeping dully into the man's angular young cheeks. Jealousy touched Scott. He had forgotten how she affected other men. Then he knew what a damned fool he was. How could a man be jealous of something he didn't have?

Jade looked up as Scott nudged his horse free of the crowd. She introduced him to Kane, and Scott acknowledged with a nod, then spoke to her.

"I thought I told you not to come."

Her chin lifted. "You're not my boss." Then she relented, her eyes darkening. "I had to, Scott. I took the short cut over the ridge. You weren't on the road and I thought you were ahead. Mister Kane's been in front of the saloon a while and he hasn't seen Yankee come in."

Scott looked about him in the crowd, tense, waiting for something, he wished he knew what. "You know what this is about?" he asked Kane.

"I understand it's over Cheyenne Parks," Kane said.

"Is the railroad going through there?"

The man shook his head. "A couple of miles south."

"What would happen if the railroad *was* going through Cheyenne Parks and a man had clear title to the land?"

Kane looked puzzled. "I guess they'd have to buy him out."

"Big money?"

"That depends. What are you getting at?"

"A man on the inside, Kane. A man who might know something. A man who always likes to get the biggest, best slice of the pie before anybody else comes along."

He was looking at the saloon as he said it, and it brought a belligerent look to Kane's face. He said: "Bannack wouldn't do anything like that. This saloon is legitimate. A lot of us out in front take a flyer. I speculated on half a dozen town lots before there was a building in Laramie."

"And maybe on the route the train would take?"

Anger brought a white ridge of flesh around Kane's compressed lips. Before he could speak, Noah appeared, shoving his horse recklessly through the crowd. "Yankee's horse is in the alley," he said.

Scott glanced at Jade, then swung off his horse, dropping the reins over the rack. To Kane, as he passed, he said: "Forget what I said. Just keep her out here."

Scott and Feather went inside, and Noah followed them. If Yankee was here, he had already gone upstairs. They pushed through the crowd till they

56

reached the foot of the stairs. A big half-breed leaned indolently against the banister, blocking their way. He had a three-inch belly gun stuck in the hip pocket of his linsey-woolsey jeans and he was picking at his animal-white teeth with the tip of a clasp knife.

"Mister Bannack ain't in today, gents. Out on a survey or something."

"I thought Kalispel usually did this sort of thing," Scott said.

"He's out getting his busted ribs taped up."

"You let Yankee through."

"Yankee, gents?"

"Farmer type, white-headed, soot all over this clothes."

"Ah." The half-breed closed his clasp knife with a soft snap. "Bannack told me he could go up."

"Then Bannack's here."

"Let's say Yankee's got business. Let's say you ain't."

Scott knew they couldn't afford to wait. "Noah," he said.

Noah glanced at him, then started to circle the half-breed. The man stiffened and his attention swung to Noah for that instant. Scott kicked him in the knee. He howled and doubled forward, pawing for the belly gun. Noah caught his elbow and pulled him against the banister so hard it cracked beneath his weight and spilled him over into a short card table, upsetting the table and sliding the half-breed off into the laps of a pair of players.

57

The three brothers rushed up the stairs. The office door was open and Scott could hear Yankee's voice, brittle, shrill, near the breaking point.

"Step out from behind that desk, Bannack."

Scott was first through the door. He saw Bannack in the room, by his swivel chair, and Riordan standing over by the window. Yankee heard Scott behind him and wheeled. His fists were clenched and repressed rage was stamped into his whitened face like a brand.

"What the hell is this?" Bannack asked Scott. "You better get him out of here and sober him up."

Yankee wheeled back. His voice sounded crazy. "I'm not drunk. Are you getting out from behind that desk or do you want me to pull my gun?"

One of Bannack's eyes was swollen completely shut. There was a deep gash over the other brow. His lips were split and puffed out and the flesh across his cheeks was red as raw meat from the beating he had sustained this morning. Perhaps he was remembering that beating, as he glanced at Yankee's hand, like a sinewy claw above the butt of his gun.

"Pa," Scott said, "take it easy. . . ."

"Don't tell me what to do," Yankee said. "I've got him dead to rights. You think I'm going to let him off now? Move, Bannack."

Still Bannack hesitated. Scott saw Yankee's hand trembling above the gun and was afraid to move. In that moment, his eyes focused on Bannack—a man who had ridden with Quantrill. He was the most controversial figure to come out of the War Between the

States, vilified by some, defied by others, hated by North and South alike. Knowing allegiance to neither cause, Quantrill used the war as an excuse to raid and loot and terrorize, dressing his brigands in gray and raiding a town on the Union side, wearing blue and raping a town with Southern sympathies. Scott had seen the towns he had burned, the women his men had ravished. If this was truly Bannack's background, Scott could almost understand Yankee's fanatical hatred.

"Bannack?" Yankee's voice sounded strangled.

Slowly, reluctantly, Bannack moved from behind the desk. Yankee's eyes dropped to his pants, held tight beneath the instep by a strap. Then Yankee's eyes slid around to Scott. They were tinged with blood in the corners and shining like a wild animal's.

"You wanted proof," he said. "Where would he get red mud on his boots? The only clay bog I've seen around here is on the creekbank behind our barn."

Riordan tried that bland smile. "We stopped by your place to ask where you could be found . . . this morning."

"The hell you did!" Noah said. "I was there. Nobody stopped."

Bannack started to protest. There was a tramping sound on the stairs and someone's voice raised in a shout. The tension went out of Bannack's face and he settled back, split lips grinning balefully.

"So your shack was burned," he said. "If I was you, Yankee, I'd take that as sort of a warning. A lot worse things could happen to a man."

59

Yankee began to tremble. "You admit it. You admit it to my face."

"That's what I'd do," Bannack told him. "I'd take it as sort of a warning. Maybe that's what you did. You realized a lot worse things could happen to a man, and you come in to keep them from happening. You come in to sign that lease. . . ."

"That half-breed's coming up," Feather said. "He's got men with him."

Yankee didn't seem to hear. With a sound of rage he leaped at Bannack. The man dodged behind the desk, pulling for his gun.

"I won't take it again, Yankee. You won't lay a hand on me. . . ."

Yankee threw himself across the desk at the man. Bannack got his gun and sent the bullet wild. Bannack spun away, and Yankee slid past him and spilled off onto the floor.

As Bannack staggered backward, lifting his gun to fire again at Yankee, Scott drew his Colt and shot the man. Bannack's face went blank with shock. He stiffened, spun around, and then sat down hard against the wall.

A gun leaped into Riordan's hand and he started to fire at Scott. But Noah's gun made a deafening smash beside Scott's hip, and Riordan stiffened against the wall, his face a mask of pain. While he still hung there, Yankee got to his feet behind the desk. His gun was drawn and he ran from behind the desk and fired pointblank at Riordan again.

60

It was a shocking sight, that white-haired man firing into the helpless Irishman, holding him against the wall and firing his gun into him. When the weapon was empty, Yankee flung it from him and whirled around. Seeing Bannack's gun on the floor, he scooped it up.

Scott realized what he intended. He lunged across the room. As Yankee raised the gun to fire at Bannack, who sat, helpless and wounded, against the wall, Scott hit his father across the back of the neck with his own weapon.

With Yankee pitching forward, Scott heard the blare of Noah's gun from the balcony outside. Scott saw that Noah had run out to the railing and was firing down the stairs. Feather stood in the doorway, held there by shock and indecision. Noah looked back over his shoulder, saw Yankee on the floor, and shouted: "I can hold them a minute! Get him out the back way."

Scott got his father under the arms and started dragging him toward the door. He shouted at Feather who jerked, as if coming out of a trance, and ran past him to the door.

"It's locked, Scott."

"Shoot it off. Use your head."

Riordan lay in a heap on the floor, blood staining the raw planks beneath him. Bannack sat against the wall, eyes closed with pain, gripping the wound in his shoulder with both hands.

Feather's shots smashed the lock, and he tore the door open. A bullet whined past Noah and hit the window. Glass shattered in a thousand pieces, spilling all over Scott. He and Feather dragged Yankee downstairs. At the bottom, Yankee began to come to. Scott sat him on the bottom step and called: "Noah . . . ?" His voice boomed up the hollow, covered stairway and Scott heard the clatter of Noah's feet in the room above. He turned to Feather, speaking swiftly: "Go around front. Bring the horses. Get Jade up and going."

Feather nodded, white-faced, and turned to run. Scott helped Yankee to his feet. He didn't want to think about what had happened, or question why he should help him, why he should want to save him, after what had happened. This man was his father. It was all he should know, all he should think. Above everything else, this man was his father, and he owed him that much—this man was his father: he tried to hold that in his mind, blotting out the rest, his father, his father. . . .

Yankee's face was slack and gray. He looked spent, and his glazed eyes fought for comprehension. Scott pushed him toward his horse, still standing hipshot and rimed with drying lather, halfway down the alley.

Noah came running down the stairway behind them. "I got that 'breed." He stopped by Yankee, staring at him. "I thought you were hit."

"I did it," Scott said grimly.

Noah gaped at him. "What the hell?"

There was the drum of hoofs at the alley mouth and Feather appeared, herding the other two horses before him. Scott pushed Yankee to his horse and Noah helped him heave the dazed man aboard. Then they turned the animal and slapped its rump. It went stumbling down the alley. Somebody was shouting and running down the stairs behind them. Feather had already driven their animals to them, and they swung aboard, heading down the alley after Yankee, away from the main street. Jade came up on Scott's flank, mounted on the black.

As they reached the other end of the alley, the man ran out of the covered stairway and took a shot at them. Scott and Jade were last in line, and they wheeled around the corner with the bullet slamming into a wall ten feet behind them.

They ran blindly through a maze of muddy back yards and alleys. Jade ran her winded horse beside Scott, calling breathlessly: "What is it? What happened?"

Scott looked at her, miserable and helpless. He couldn't answer.

CHAPTER SIX

Eagle Gap was deep in the Laramie Mountains, thirty miles from the Fetterman Cut-Off or any other main route of travel, reached by the faintest of game trails that climbed the pine-covered slopes to enter the narrow gap sliced eons ago through the solid granite of a great ridge. To the west the stands of pine and spruce formed dark and shaggy shoulders that fell off

63

at last into parks of wild hay blown by the wind into a glittering emerald ocean.

The Walkers reached the gap near dawn, having ridden the night through. Noah's horse went down as they entered the notch. It was wind-broken, ruined, and they all knew they would have to shoot it. Scott dropped off his own quivering, groaning animal and stumbled to the rocks beneath the gray potholed cliff. He lowered himself to the ground and leaned against a moss-covered boulder, so exhausted he couldn't think.

One by one the others followed, dropping to the ground, stupid with weariness. Only Yankee kept his feet, standing silhouetted against the pearly dawn in the mouth of the gap and staring off at the wilderness behind them. Feather sat against a rock with his head lolling back and his mouth slack with exhaustion. Finally he looked at Scott, still shocked and unable to comprehend the sudden, inexplicable course of violence that had torn their lives apart in the last twenty-four hours.

"Think they'll follow us?" he asked.

"That town?" Noah said disgustedly. "They don't even have a marshal."

"They've got the vigilance committee."

Scott roused himself with an effort. "The what?"

"The town wasn't incorporated," Feather said. "There wasn't any law. Things got so bad a bunch of railroaders and shopkeepers organized this committee. They strung a man up last week for a shooting."

64

Scott was frowning now, trying to think clearly. "Bannack was with the railroad, wasn't he?"

"He worked for the government," Noah said.

"That makes it worse," Scott said. "They won't let this go."

Feather's eyes shone. "You think them vigilantes will be after us?"

"Shut up, all of you," Yankee said. His voice broke in on them like a thunderclap, making them all look sharply toward him. He stood with his narrow shoulders tight and high, his fists clenched. "What we did was right and proper. When they find out what Bannack did to us, they'll know we were justified. He was a scoundrel, a thief, and a murderer. He should have been killed like the hound he was years ago when they cleaned out the rest of Quantrill's gang."

Scott looked at the man. Could Yankee actually find justification in what he had done? Maybe Feather was right. The Quantrill burning had really twisted Yankee. Or maybe it had always been there—in the unyielding stubbornness, the blind pride, the dogmatic concepts, the ungovernable rage—waiting to take shape in something like this. Why were children so accepting of those things? They had seemed a natural part of the man, in Scott's boyhood. It was an age of stern fathers. To them, he had been honest, God-fearing, a pillar of the community, hard-working almost to the point of obsession. How could it all take such different shape now?

Scott shook his head. He was too exhausted to find

65

the sources. After four years of war he had thought he couldn't be shocked by anything. But this had left him reeling. He felt totally unable to cope with it. He had lost all contact with Yankee.

Jade's voice came to him, feeble, hopeless. "We've got to rest. We can't go any farther without rest."

Yankee turned. His eyes were feverish-looking and red-rimmed. There was a stubble of beard growth on his face and it gave a senile look to the deep lines about his mouth.

"We'll stand watch. Scott, you take the first two hours. Then wake me up."

He waited, as if he expected a protest. Scott didn't speak. He didn't think he could sleep anyway, with that picture of Riordan in his mind, that picture of Yankee's berserk face.

While the others stripped their rigging off and used the saddle blankets, sweaty as they were, for covering, Scott walked around the turn in the gap and stopped above Noah's horse. It was lying on its side, breathing in little whimpering sounds, a pitiful, ruined beast. The only merciful thing was to kill it. He took out his gun. He didn't want to do it. But he had to. The animal was incapable of foraging for itself. It would starve. The quick way was the best. He bent down, put the muzzle to its head.

The shot smashed out into empty air. He turned away, sick inside, and walked down the cliff till he was out of sight of the horse and of the others. He sat down with his back against the cliff. He found makings in his pocket and rolled a cigarette. He closed his eyes and tried not to think, tried not to look beyond the next second.

He sank slowly into a sort of stupor, neither waking nor sleeping, and lost all measure of time. It seemed hours before a sound roused him. He saw Jade picking her way through the shale toward him.

"The others are asleep, I guess," she said.

"You should be, too."

"I couldn't."

She stood above him, looking down with a numb misery in her face. Her dress was torn and soiled and her hair was matted and bedraggled and smudges of soot still smeared her cheeks, yet it could hide none of her beauty from him. The vivid softness of lips and the taut mold of her upthrust breasts and the curve of her lips all blocked the breath poignantly in his throat.

"Scott," she said. Her voice was weak and hopeless. "What's happened? I saw it all, but I can't believe it. I can't understand it. I feel like I'm in a nightmare or something and it's going to end any minute . . . it's got to end."

He rose. The motion stopped her and stifled what had been the beginnings of hysteria. He rolled another cigarette, lighting it on his own.

"The world falls in on you sometimes, Jade," he said. "I thought I'd learned to take it during the war." He handed her the cigarette. She hesitated. "You used to sneak corn shucks with me out behind the barn," he said.

67

She took the cigarette. "I still take a puff on Noah's once in a while. When Yankee isn't looking."

"Little thing like that helps sometimes," he said. "I don't know why."

She closed her eyes, taking a deep drag. "It does," she whispered.

For a moment it was six years ago, one of their little conspiracies against Yankee, or the boys, their magic circle that held them apart and hid them from the rest of the world. Then Jade opened her eyes and showed him her misery again.

"Scott," she said, "what will we do?"

He did not speak for a moment. Then, looking out into an empty distance, he answered. "I guess we'll run. What else does a killer do?"

"But we're not killers." She was pleading, with herself, with him, with all the frightening unknown forces that had forced them into this dark corner. "You didn't kill anybody. It was Yankee."

"They'll think of us as sort of a gang now," he said bitterly. "The Walker gang. All there when Riordan was killed."

"It was self-defense. Riordan had his gun. . . ."

"It was murder, Jade. It was cold-blooded murder." *And my father did it*. Almost as if he'd said it. The words, in his mind, were like sounds, like echoes, something he could hear and say and wanted to grasp, wanted to comprehend, and couldn't comprehend.

He threw his cigarette from him. He was being a fool, a child. He had to face up to this. He couldn't wander around in a daze any longer. He had to see it for what it was and make a decision for himself, for all of them.

He looked at her. How could all that pain still be in him, that wanting? The world had come to pieces and all he could think of was that need for her, whenever she was near, that aching need.

"It's crazy," he said. "Yesterday I thought the worst had happened. I thought the biggest question I'd ever face was just you and me."

She put her hand to her eyes. "Seems sort of small now, doesn't it?"

"Does it?"

She lowered her hand slowly. Her eyes were dark and bottomless. She swayed, and he thought she would come to him. The cigarette slipped from her fingers and a low moan left her lips. The rattle of shale checked whatever she would have done.

Noah was making his way precariously around the curving cliff. He stopped. Suspicion was in his haggard face. He looked at them for a long time before he spoke.

"You make a fine watchman," he said. He glanced down the mountain. "They're almost on us."

Scott glanced sharply down the long, steep shoulder of the mountain and saw what his attention on Jade had kept him from seeing: A file of riders was laboring up the game trail, like toy figures at such a great distance. A dark-faced Indian was walking at the stirrup of the leader, studying every foot of the ground traversed, pointing out tracks. That leader, even at this distance, was recognizable—a tall, broad-shouldered man in khaki with a bright red bandanna knotted around his neck.

"It's Kane," Scott said. "Harvey Kane."

"And the vigilance committee," Noah said huskily. "Shall we wait for 'em to light and set a while, or are you comin'?"

Scott caught Jade's arm, hurrying her alongside of him as he started for the gap. Noah wheeled ahead of them. Once in the gap, Scott saw that Feather and Noah already had three horses saddled. The kid was throwing Scott's rig aboard the single-foot.

"How many are there?" Yankee asked.

"About a dozen," Noah answered.

Yankee hesitated.

Noah said viciously: "We can't make a stand. We ain't got a chance. We ain't even got saddle guns."

Yankee's face turned pale and his eyes blazed at Noah. He waved his arm in a dictatorial gesture.

"Noah, you ride Jade's horse. She can get up behind. If we get separated, meet at Rawlins Springs."

Feather tugged Scott's latigo tight and tucked the end into a cinch ring, looking up at Scott with a pinched face. Scott clapped him on the shoulder.

"Stick with it, kid. We'll be all right."

They filed through the narrow notch. The trail led out onto a bald slope toward dense timber on the lower shoulders. The mountains rolled away like an endless sea, bearded black with fir and pine, and it

70

seemed as though once a man was in that illimitable forest he could lose himself from the world. Scott knew what an illusion that was, with that Indian tracker behind them.

They walked their animals into the first timber and the chill made Scott shiver. Yankee was looking about him, lips working, as if trying to make a decision.

"A half a mile of running would finish these horses," Scott said.

Yankee glanced sharply at him, and for the first time his eyes showed confusion. "We got to do something."

"Just keep ahead of them," Scott answered. "It's all we can do. Keep ahead and out of sight. Maybe come night we can lose them."

"That Indian'll see how fresh this sign is." Noah's voice was brittle with tension.

"Their animals are tired, too," Scott said. "Chances are they won't rush it unless they see us."

They rode through the growing heat of noon, through a sun-hazed afternoon, through a wind that came booming up like a surf near evening, prodding failing mounts. They halted on the ridges to look back and see that file of riders behind them, following doggedly, gradually narrowing the gap. They found a stream and used it to hide their tracks but it didn't help. The vigilantes divided and the group with the tracker was lucky enough to choose the upstream direction the Walkers had taken so that, when the Walkers had to leave the creek at the headwaters, the Indian was there to find the sign.

71

Unable to stop. Unable to rest on their horses for a moment. So stupid with exhaustion that just before nightfall Feather went to sleep and fell out of his saddle. It was the same exhaustion that betrayed them all in the end.

Scott was riding drag and he kept halting at the high points to keep a check on their trailers. Just after nightfall they crossed a ridge and he stopped and let them go on.

He wanted to sleep so badly it was like pain. He kept nodding forward in the saddle. His brain was drugged and there wasn't much will left in him to hold on. He knew Kane and his men and their animals were just as played out. They were following doggedly, unwilling to spend their animals in a last burst, bent on wearing the Walkers down. It was an old practice for the manhunter. It was the end of a long, long game. . . .

Scott jerked in his saddle. Had he dozed? He looked about him. There was a soft snapping on his flank and he shook his head, trying to sharpen his dulled faculties, pulling his gun. A squirrel rustled through pine needles, and he relaxed, the sweat cold on his forehead.

The squirrel made another rustling. Only it wasn't to his left this time. Delayed reaction made him turn, pull up his gun. He saw the shadowy figure parting the bushes not twenty yards from him.

It was the Indian. He saw Scott, shouted, ducked back into the bushes. Scott's first impulse was to fire but he checked it with effort. The shout had reached the others and he heard them in a burst of sound—the rattle of hoofs laboring upward through shale, the wheeze of driven horses. He wheeled his mount and put it into a run.

The animal stumbled, almost fell, and Scott had to pull him down to keep from getting pitched off. At the same time the riders charged over the ridge behind.

They opened fire. It panicked his horse. The animal was so exhausted that even the frenzy of fear couldn't keep it on its feet. It ran wild for fifty feet and then its flank struck a tree and it went down.

Scott kicked free and rolled automatically when he hit. A springy mat of pine needles broke his fall. Long habit made him hold onto his gun as he flopped over and over and finally plowed deep into a thicket.

Lying there, screened by the thicket, he saw that his horse had not been visible to those behind. The ground trembled beneath Scott as their horses rushed past, chasing the riderless horse that fled ahead of them.

As soon as the mounted men had passed, Scott started to roll over. Then he froze as the *thud* of more hoofs came to him. It was the Indian. He had mounted his own horse and was tailing the others. He, too, raced by without seeing Scott.

Deep in the timber ahead guns began to crash once more. Sickly Scott knew that Kane had caught up with the other Walkers. He got to his feet and ran toward the sound. It receded from him—the wild shooting and the crash of guns and the thunder of running horses—till it seemed to be at a great distance.

He could run no longer and had to stop, with the breath pounding through him. The firing became sporadic, and finally ceased. He halted, listening, hearing nothing. He couldn't believe it would end so quickly. Had the Walkers somehow eluded Kane?

Warily he began moving down through the timber. He knew that the vigilantes had been forced to divide when the Walkers took to that stream, for he had counted only half a dozen of them whenever he had sighted them this afternoon. There weren't enough men really to cover the Walkers, if they had the sense to split up. It was his only hope.

In half an hour he had reached the bottom of a deep cañon. As far as he could judge, this was where the firing ceased. If they had been caught, it was here. If they had split up and gone on, he could not hope to catch them.

He climbed among some rocks, covering his sign as best he could, and settled down to wait for daylight. It would tell him the story. He spent the night in a stupor, waking countless times with a start, dreaming of Atlanta and hearing the siege guns again. The sun on his face woke him.

He was dizzy with hunger, parched with thirst, and nauseated. When he moved, he had to retch, but there was nothing to come up. Finally he made it down to the bottom of the cañon again and hunted painstakingly, doggedly, for sign, till he found it. By hoof prints in wet clay he could see that the Walkers had come into the cañon bottom at a run and split up, each horse taking a different direction. Kane's men had fol-lowed. Apparently they hadn't seen the split and all of them had taken out after one of the Walkers, thinking they were still after all three.

Scott followed the trail to a ridge and lost it in the shale. From this height he could see a vast stretch of primitive forest. The mountains seemed to drop away from his very feet. The mass of trees was broken here and there by sweeping meadows or mountain parks.

It was a vast and awesome sight and it produced a loneliness in him like an unbearable pressure. He knew that if any of the Walkers had escaped, he was powerless to find them afoot. It was what he had to concentrate on now.

Thinking of Jade, he felt sick. He clenched his fists and looked up at the sky and wanted to cry with his impotence. Then he shook his head helplessly. If she had escaped, there was only one way he could find out now. It had to do with what Yankee had said there in Eagle Gap, should they become separated.

Rawlins Springs.

CHAPTER SEVEN

All the spring of 1868 the Union Pacific tracks had crawled westward across Nebraska and Wyoming— Omaha, Kearney, North Platte, Julesburg, Cheyenne, and finally Laramie. One by one, as the rails reached the towns, they bloomed, like some exotic flower for a few weeks, then faded as the rails marched on.

Those rails were fifteen miles west of Laramie by the time Scott reached them again. But he didn't see the end of track at first. He tried to strike the line as close to Laramie as possible without actually returning to the town itself. The first thing he wanted, above all else, was to find out if any of the Walkers had been captured.

It had taken him three days to get back on foot through a wilderness empty of humans. The first night he killed a jack rabbit with a stone and spitted its stringy meat over a feeble blaze, eating tripe and all, and then sucking marrow from the bones. The second night he halted by a pool and spent four hours, using his hat as a net, before he snared a trout. The third night he found a tie-cutters' camp, and chanced going in. He gave only the name of Scott and told them he was one of a surveying party who had got lost. They believed the story and fed him, and from them he got the news he wanted. One of their number had been to Laramie the night before and had seen Kane and his vigilance committee return empty-handed.

76

That decided Scott. His destination was Rawlins Springs.

He struck the rails the next morning, two miles out of Laramie, and waited but half an hour before one of the construction trains passed him. It was climbing a grade and going slowly enough for him to swing on. When the brakeman came back, he said he was going out to sign on with the rail layers. Then he asked about Rawlins Springs.

The man told him it was a hundred miles beyond end of track, over nothing but mountain and desert. Scott realized he'd need a few square meals and money for a horse to get through that wilderness. The quickest way to get both would be to work on the railroad.

The train took him northwest over a vast grassland, with the Medicine Bow Mountains etching a jagged pattern against the sky in the distance. They crossed endless sage flats and ran over high plains where a wind came out of the mountains and swept stinging sand across the tracks. Finally, in a rugged and broken country, they came to the end of the rails.

Scott had seen the beginnings of the railroad at Omaha, but the unholy welter of men and material surrounding end of track never ceased to amaze him. Here, in an area of a few square miles, five thousand men were at work tearing up the land and driving a steel highway across a continent. A pall of dust lay like smoke over the horizon, raised by a thousand grading teams laboring with their plows and scrapers. Disappearing into that dust were the rails, flanked by a vast array of groaning Murphy wagons and six-hitch mule teams and sweating bullwhackers freighting in supplies, heaps of ties and rails dumped for use, sleeping cars eighty feet long, and rolling kitchens switched off to spurs, and hundreds of tents and makeshift shelters spread out across the plain as far as a man could see.

Ahead of the train a handcar piled with gleaming rails and burnetized ties was clattering down toward the end. Waiting for it were the track layers, hundreds of them, stripped to the waist, dripping sweat, dragging the rails off the handcar onto rollers and spiking them down with a *clank* of sledges that was never still. It was an awesome sight, and for a moment it filled Scott with a sense of appalling insignificance and wiped his own trouble from his mind.

The brakemen began making their precarious way across the loaded flats and setting their brakes. The whole train started lurching and shrieking and clanking as it ground to a halt. As the three cars in Scott's section rolled onto a spur, he dropped off and made his way toward the first crew of track layers. They were already unloading rails from the flat onto a smaller handcar, shouting and cursing and shining with perspiration. Scott asked one where the section boss was. Without even looking at him, the man waved toward the end of track.

"Sean Quinn, little gossoon with the rid whiskers."

Scott walked down the track, so weak with hunger it was a great effort to move. He was sweating and dizzy by the time he saw the bowlegged bantam with the red beard. He wore a pair of immense brogans, linsey-woolsey jeans held up by a pair of crimson galluses, his long underwear sufficing for a shirt, its sleeves rolled elbow high to expose a pair of freckled forearms tufted with fuzzy red hair. He had a clay pipe clamped between his teeth and the rank smell of the tobacco almost knocked Scott over while he was still ten feet away.

"Sean Quinn?" Scott asked.

"Mister Quinn t'you," the man said. He made a violent gesture with one arm and squealed like a pig. "Git those chairs down, y'mor Dubh-gaills, there's a new load a-comin' and I'll crown y'r pates with every rail y'fall behind."

A new flurry ran through the crew, and the *clang* of sledges increased in tempo.

Scott said: "They told me at Laramie you could use more rail layers."

"Whoosh!" Quinn said. He waved his arm again. "That spike's crooked, Burke. Ye wanna be docked a pint o' tay?" He had not looked at Scott yet. "Been t' Cork?" he asked.

"No," Scott said.

"Athlone?"

"No."

"Galway?"

"No."

79

"What kind of Irishman are ye?"

"I'm afraid not at all." Scott hesitated. He knew how dangerous the name Walker might be. "Scott's the name."

"Sir Walter Scott was an Irishman. His grandmother went over from Balbriggan and married one o' them Finn gaills on the border."

"I never heard that."

Quinn turned, pipe still clamped between his teeth. He took Scott by the jaw, tilting his head up and down, from side to side. "Gaelic as a stook of oats," he said. "Couldn't be nothing else. Black, loquacious, tale-telling, of a low and groveling mind. I kin tell 'em every time. A Firbolg, that's what ye are, right out of Dun Aenghus."

"That I'll be," Scott said, "if it'll get me the job."

Quinn hit him on the shoulder. "Not much muscle. Ain't tryin' t'bum a meal off me, are ye?"

"I'll admit I'm hungry."

"Ye'll work before ye eat."

"I counted on it."

"And if ye do, ye'll pass out," Quinn said.

Scott looked surprised.

Quinn took his pipe from his mouth and laughed. "*Whoosh!* I never saw such a pale malrach. How long since you've set down to a decent meal?"

"A few days."

Quinn tamped tobacco into his pipe. "I was broke once and a man named Casement give me a meal before I wint t'work and I been rich ever since. Go down to the kitchen car now and git a bellyful and come back ready t'sweat."

Scott wended his way through the tangle, dodging teams of mules and lurching wagons, picking his way around heaps of ties, plows, and scrapers. At last he reached the kitchen car on a spur, a flat eighty feet long on which had been built a shanty with half a dozen tin chimneys poking from its roof. The chief cook was a potbellied man with glowing red cheeks and a pair of hands like hams.

"Quinn sent me for a meal," Scott said.

The man was busy dumping peeled potatoes into a huge stew kettle. "How do I know?"

"He thinks Sir Walter Scott was an Irishman."

The man nodded. "Yerra, that's Quinn." He glared at Scott suddenly. "Do y'doubt it?"

"Not for a minute. His grandmother went over from Balbriggan and married one o' them Finn gaills on the border."

"That she did. Are you a Connacht man?"

"No."

"Y'look like a Connacht man." The cook shouted at one of the men peeling potatoes on a bench. "Dish up some spuds for this one! Some o' that beef we had left over, too. If there's any pie in the box, he can finish it."

Scott fell to with a will.

As he made his way back toward end of track, Scott passed a row of sleeping cars on a spur. In front of one a dozen poles were planted in the ground, carrying lines loaded with laundry. The engine down the track began hooting madly. On every side men dropped their sledges and swarmed toward the kitchen cars. He was completely unprepared for the first rush of them. A giant on the edge of the mob rammed into his shoulder, spinning him helplessly into the laundry. His flailing arms hooked on one of the lines as he fell, pulling it down with him. The first pole was pulled across another line, uprooting a second pole, and it fell across a third line, and the whole network began going down like a house of cards.

When it was over, he lay beneath a heap of rope and stakes and clothing. As he tried to fight his way out of it, he heard someone screaming like a banshee.

"Oh, ye mor muck, who filled ye with porter in the middle o' the day, who gave ye leave t'be staggerin' around in a dayc'nt God-fearin' woman's front yard and spilin' a whole day's work?" He grunted, as something hit him across the belly. He tried to roll away. His face was still wrapped up in clothes. He couldn't see a thing. More blows descended upon him. "I'll have the Quinn down on ye, that's what I'll do. I'll have him dock y'r drunken Irish face so I can lambaste it good an' proper an' send ye up to the Quinn with the marks of infamy showin' right out in broad daylight . . . !"

He finally unwound a pair of man's long underwear from around his head and saw her. She stood before him, a red-haired fury in a man's white shirt and a voluminous wool skirt, her blue eyes blazing, her face so red the freckles hardly showed on her snub nose, her hair wild and tousled as a wind-blown bonfire. He knew who it was now.

She struck at him with the mop handle again, and he avoided it, rolling aside and coming to his feet with underwear and shirts and pants trailing from his shoulders and arms. He backed up, arms in front of his face, as she swung once more, still yelling shrilly.

"I'll teach ye t'be drinkin' y'r lunch. I'll spike ye down with y'r next rail. I'll. . . ."

"Hold on, Miss Quinn," he said. He was laughing. "I couldn't help it. I'm not drunk. That gang of wild men charged by and some big Mick with a cigar knocked me off my feet."

She had him backed up against the car. She stopped, a blank look coming to her face. "You!" she said. She sounded incredulous, shocked, and apoplectic all at once. He knew she couldn't have seen him that night.

"I'm flattered you remember my words," he said.

"Remember? How could I forget? Whaddaya think the Quinn did when I showed up with a wagonload of mud in my flour? My backsides are still red." She straightened. "Bend over."

"What?"

"If anybody gets a larrupin' this time, it's gonna be you, with five thousand witnesses as to jist who's responsible for this devastation."

"How is it we always seem fated to meet under such ridiculous circumstances?"

"Ridiculous, is it?"

"Wait a minute, now." He held his hands up to stop the incipient tirade. "While you're still calm, isn't there some other way I can pay for my sins? I'll be working. Half of each day's pay?"

"All y'r pay wouldn't put the clothes on these men's backs where they're supposed t'be." She looked miserably around at the laundry, lying in soiled heaps on the ground. The sight brought raging tears to her eyes, and she wheeled on him in a new outburst. "Ye've put me behind a week. I'll never catch up." She lifted the mop. "Oh, ye moke, ye stupid, bumblin' gombeen man . . . !"

He dodged the blow, holding up his hands again. "Wait, now, I have another suggestion."

When Sean Quinn and his bully boys marched back from the kitchen cars to work, they saw the sight. They stopped, a dozen of them, then a score, then half a hundred, gaping like fools. Quinn elbowed his way through, staring, making motions with his mouth. One of the men spat.

"I thought ye said he was a Connacht man."

"The cook said he was a Connacht man," another answered.

"He couldn't be a Connacht man. No Connacht man'd do that."

"Quiet!" It came from Quinn in that shrill squeal and brought instantaneous silence. He stepped forward, spread his feet, swayed his back, put his thumbs in his galluses, and cleared his throat. "I'm glad ye found a way to pay for y'r meal," he told Scott, "because I'd hate t'give y'the sack with a free lunch in y'r belly."

Penny appeared at the door of the sleeping car, a mop in her hand. "Fire him and ye'll have no clothes."

Quinn's red brows rose in surprise and a disturbed murmur ran through the men. Scott stood helplessly by the washtub. He had taken off his shirt and his arms were covered with suds to the shoulders. He felt like a fool and he knew he was blushing. Damn all those grinning Hibernians.

"The way I see it," Penny said, "it ain't really his fault. All ye stupid malrachs come chargin' by like Paddy to a wake and knocked him head over heels into my washin'. He said some big Mick with a cigar. That'd be you, Mickey Dan."

Mickey Dan stood six foot two, weighed more than two hundred pounds, all muscle, and must have measured a long axe handle through the shoulders. He had curly black hair and a jaw that would always have a steel-blue shadow no matter how often he shaved. A hurt look came to his broad and craggy face and he removed the frayed cigar from his lips.

"Beggin' y'r pardon, Penny Quinn, but I never knocked a man from his feet in me life without the usual formalities. And I haven't even been introduced to this fine broth of a boy."

A great hoot went up from the gang and Quinn smiled complacently. Penny shook the mop at Mickey Dan.

85

"His name is Scott and ye can join him right now in his ablutions."

Quinn snapped his galluses officiously. "Hold on, me darlin', I can't have Mickey Dan off my crew. We'd lose a mile a day."

"He's responsible for this mess," she said. "It's either that or be a week behind in y'r wash."

One by one the men looked at Mickey Dan. He seemed to shrink beneath the weight of their condemnation. Quinn shook his head sadly.

"Yerra, it looks like y'r doomed, Mickey Dan. We'd be the laughingstock o' the road if t'was known that Sean Quinn's whole crew worked a week without their under-drawers."

CHAPTER EIGHT

With dark, the crews swarmed back to the kitchen cars again, passing the two men at the washtubs. They stopped to hoot and jeer and make rough jokes that Scott couldn't understand. Finally the washing was done and Scott dried off with a towel and donned his shirt. Penny Quinn was not in sight, and the two men walked to the kitchen fires together. Mickey Dan was rolling down his sleeves, surveying Scott's height with a critical eye.

"Five feet, eleven inches," he said.

"Six feet even," Scott said.

"Twelve stone."

"How much is a stone?"

"Fourteen pounds."

"Then you're three pounds off. What's all this for?"

"I always like to size a man up before I fight 'im."

"You fight all the new men?"

"Sooner or later. In this case you brought it on sooner. You shamed me before the whole crew. I'll have to lick every last one of 'em all over again. And I'm tired tonight."

"Why don't we eat first?"

"I'd planned on it."

Scott had known plenty of this kind in the Army. Like children, with their simple emotions and their simple lives. Quick to anger and as quick to forget it. He didn't want to fight Mickey Dan because he liked the man. He hoped a heavy meal would make the man mellower.

A hundred campfires bloomed around the kitchen cars and the crews were already eating, seated on cross-ties or piles of rails or on the ground. It was a prodigious meal—soup, meat, potatoes, pan bread, canned peaches, dried-apple pie, and coffee. After it was over and all the dishes were in the wreck pan, Mickey Dan threw away his frayed stub, got a fresh cigar from his pocket, lit it at one of the fires, and climbed atop a pile of ties.

"You still got soap in y'r ears, Missus Briggs," someone shouted.

"Exactly what I wanted to make an announcement about," Mickey Dan said. "First, I am going to whip Mister Scott. Then I'll take on the rest o' you, one at a time. At a minit apiece, I figure that will let me get to bed by midnight. Now, if you'll form a line on the right, I'll prepare to accommodate you. And please try not to knock me cigar out of me mouth."

Hooting and shouting like a gang of schoolboys, they started jumping to their feet. Before half of them were up, there was the muted tinkle of accouterments and a lieutenant of cavalry rode into the mob, firelight winking against the yellow stripes on his blue pants.

"Douse your fires," he said. "You're just making targets down here. Get to the cars and keep your guns handy. It looks like a bad night."

The transformation was startling. Without a lost motion the men forgot Mickey Dan, stopped yelling, and turned to kick out the fires. In the space of thirty seconds there wasn't a light in the whole area. Scott stood ten feet from Mickey Dan as the man dropped off the ties.

"This way," he said. "The Quinn's crew has three cars on that spur beyond the kitchens."

Like well-trained platoons, each crew was separating from the main mob and running to its respective sleeping cars. Sean Quinn led his hundred men at a dog-trot past the kitchens. "Out with that cigar," he told Mickey Dan. "You wanna go without y'r tay tomorrer?"

Mickey Dan jammed the cigar against his shirt and then stuffed it back into his mouth. They reached the cars, and a dozen men climbed inside and began handing out the rifles. It was a new gun to Scott and he checked the action in the darkness.

"Looks like a breechloader."

"Spencer," Mickey Dan said. "A good gun."

"This a cartridge tube in the butt?"

"Seven shots."

"You do better than the Army."

"We ought to. Every redskin west o' the Missouri is tryin' to stop us from goin' through."

The men all had their guns now and Quinn dropped out of the car, saying: "The lieutenant don't know whether they're comin' in yet or not. Keep close t'the cars till bedtime. If anything happens, there's extra cartridge tubes in the car and a pair o' men to hand 'em out. Now settle down, an' no smokes."

Ties had already been piled in cribs all around the cars and the men took their positions behind these makeshift breastworks. Quinn joined Mickey Dan and Scott, peering off across the broken country.

"I don't see nothin'," Mickey Dan said.

"Ye won't," Quinn told him, "till they come in. Lieutenant Lawler said his scouts spotted them from that northward rise. Big party all painted up."

A figure dropped softly out of the sleeping car. It was Penny. She must have come with the others but Scott had missed her in the rush. He saw a rifle in the crook of her elbow. As she joined them, Quinn said: "Back in the car with ye."

"The divil, I will," she said. "If men can wash clothes, a woman can fight Indians."

Quinn subsided, muttering to himself. Penny saw Scott looking at her and grinned impishly at him.

Mickey Dan chuckled. "She ain't half as beautiful when she's calm."

She flushed. "Then I'll raise a temper again. Quit a-gapin' and use y'r eyes fer them Indians."

"Y'know," Quinn said, "they're wrong about Sir Walter Raleigh. He never introduced the potato to Ireland."

"He was Irish, though," Scott said.

"That he was," Quinn said. "That he was."

Nothing happened that night, and after standing to their guns for an hour the crews went to the sleeping cars, leaving sentries behind the tie cribs. Scott was exhausted and fell asleep immediately in a bunk under the roof of the car. At dawn he was awakened by the cook beating on a tin basin. They rolled out, washed up, and had a breakfast fully as huge as the dinner had been. The Army escort reported no Indians in sight this morning but the crews marched out to end of track with their rifles and stacked them close at hand.

The morning train was already puffing in from Laramie, pushing a dozen long flatcars loaded with tons of iron, thousands of ties. As the crew marched back to the first flat, Quinn fell in beside Scott.

"Now y'll see what Gen'ral Jack did for us."

He explained the system that had revolutionized track laying, allowing the crews to average more than a mile a day for months. The Casement brothers, Dan

90

and Jack, had instigated it when they were given the contract for grading and rail laying in Nebraska. It was founded on having each car loaded at Omaha with a certain number of rails and the exact number of chairs and spikes required to lay them.

Before the train had halted, the men were unloading the first flat, twelve men to a rail. They piled forty of them on a handcar, with chairs and spikes. Then a teamster cracked his whip and a pair of mules hit their collars, hauling the handcar to end of track. Mickey Dan ran ahead, shirtless and sweating, and had the chocks ready to drop under the wheels as the car came to a stop at the termination of the track.

A dozen men swarmed on top of the rails and began sliding them off onto the rollers flanking the car on either side. Scott was one of the next dozen that stepped in, six to a side, and grasped the rail.

"Up with ye!" Quinn bawled. The rail came up. "Forward!" he shouted. Muscles bulging with the strain, they carried it to the grading. "Ready?" The ranks swung over till the rail was lined up. On the other side another dozen men were in line with another rail. "Down!"

The two rails dropped onto the red-cedar ties with a *clang*. The whole operation from car to ties had taken less than a minute, and the railroad was twenty-eight feet nearer the Pacific. Before the reverberations of the dropped rails had died, the mules hit their collars again, dragging the handcar over the length of the loose rails. Behind walked a man dropping chairs and spikes. Others followed, tamping the earth under the ties. Sledges flashed in silvery unison as they drove the spikes home. Scott and his crew already were by the car again, taking another rail off its rollers.

The military precision of it was surprising. It had all been reduced to a science, without a lost motion. Although it was paced to keep the men moving steadily without rushing them, Scott soon began to feel the strain. He hadn't done labor this heavy since the Army and he knew it would take him some time to find his own pace.

Mickey Dan was the moving force of Quinn's crew, doing the work of three men, prodding them constantly with his own exhibition of strength and stamina, sweating and cursing and joking all the time. He saw how Scott was tiring and took his place on the rail-laying gang.

"Drop those chairs a while. I can't have ye too tired t'fight me t'night."

Scott grinned at him and went behind the car. He was grateful for the respite. His back ached and his eyes burned and his feet felt on fire.

A detail walked their horses past with Lieutenant Lawler in the lead. He looked to be about thirty, with a heavy blond mustache that only half hid a saber scar near his mouth. He was no shave-tail with his manual in the saddlebags. Many of these lieutenants had been captains or majors three years ago, graded down after the war.

"What's the news, Lieutenant?" Quinn called.

"No sign yet," Lawler answered. "You'd better put some sentries on that rise to the north. I can't cover you all the time."

Quinn nodded and ordered a pair of men off with their Spencers. Lawler rode westward and out of sight.

In the afternoon they reached a chasm. The bridge builders had already been here and the span was waiting for the rails. There was a good drop at the center, maybe twenty feet, and a rocky streambed below. They unhitched the mules and rolled the railcar by hand. Rail by rail they moved toward the center. Twenty-eight feet. Fifty-six feet. Eighty-four feet. Like monkeys clambering around on the log trusses.

They were almost across when they saw a squad of cavalry silhouetted on the high ground to the north, where they had been posted as flankers for the rails. They were riding hard to the east and passed the sleeping cars about a thousand yards out, disappearing in a haze of their own dust. Then the other squad of flankers appeared from the south, riding in the same direction. As they raced by the sleeping car, a lone cavalryman passed them coming toward the bridge. The deafening *clank* of sledges died out gradually as more and more rail layers became aware of the troop movements. Finally Scott could hear the firing to the east.

The lone cavalryman reached Sean Quinn, standing at the end of the bridge, and pulled a lathered horse to a stop. He spoke a few sharp words to Quinn, pointed eastward. Quinn cupped his hands to his mouth, and his squealing shout rang out across the chasm.

"Come off the bridge! Them Indians hit the construction train comin' in from Laramie! Come off the bridge and stand to your guns!"

One by one and then in groups the men started to run. Some of them dropped their tools in their excitement, and a pair of sledges bounced off ties and plummeted into the chasm. Mickey Dan and Scott were both in a crew that had just dropped a rail onto the ties. They were in the extreme westward end of the line and thus were among the last men to get around the rail car and start running east down the bridge. As they ran, Scott heard a shrill and wild whooping from their right flank, and then a volley of gunfire broke against them.

One of the men ahead shouted and fell flat between the rails. Scott saw the Indians then, flooding in over the broken land to the south, their painted bodies flashing like copper pennies in the sun. In that instant Scott understood their strategy. Another party had attacked the construction train to draw the Army escort away from the bridge. Now the main body was coming in on the disorganized rail layers with no cavalry to stop it.

Mickey Dan dropped to his knee beside the fallen man, flopping him over and over. Then he rose again, shouting: "No help for that one!"

They ran on. Bullets struck the rails and the screaming howl of ricochets joined the insane babble of war cries. Quinn was like a red-whiskered madman, running toward the stacked rifles and shouting a shrill barrage of orders. A few men had already reached the Spencers and were opening up a sporadic fire on the Indians.

Then a new burst of gunfire came from behind Scott. He chanced a glance over his shoulder and saw a second bunch of Indians pulling their pinto ponies to a rearing, pirouetting stop on the opposite edge of the gorge. They were already swinging off the animals and dropping to vantage points in the rocks. Two of them ran out onto the bridge and took cover behind the rail car. Their guns smashed deafening echoes into the chasm. A bullet splintered wood from a tie at Scott's feet.

Another bullet found Mickey Dan. He and Scott were twenty feet from the end of the bridge when Mickey Dan coughed, spun around with the impact of the bullet, and pitched head over heels off the bridge. Scott was running so close behind that the falling man tripped him, and he sprawled flat on his face. He lay partially stunned. Still dazed, he made an attempt to rise to his hands and knees.

"Stay down!" It was Quinn's voice. Scott raised bleary eyes to see the red-bearded section boss crouching behind a crib of ties at the end of the bridge. "Try t'git on y'r feet and they'll cut ye in two." The crash of Quinn's Spencer punctuated his squalling voice. "Ye got t'crawl, me boy, like a snake." His rifle was smashing. "And divil a redskin that tries to poke his head up while y'r doin' it."

95

To the south, the edge of the chasm behind Scott was lower than the track bed. It was there that most of the Indians on that side had taken over. Lying down, Scott was not exposed to them. It was the pair behind the rail car that had him dead to rights. He was a sitting duck to them, and Quinn's fire, keeping them behind cover, was the only thing that kept him alive. But that Spencer held only seven shots, and Quinn was already bawling to his men for another rifle. A sun-blackened Dubliner named Con Dempsey came on the run carrying a pair of rifles.

With his heart in his mouth, Scott wormed down the ties. Bullets were still ricocheting off the rails as the Indians on the edge of the chasm sought to hit him, and he knew it was worth his life to raise his head an inch. Through each space between the ties he had a glimpse down through the log trusses into the chasm below, and he had not crawled ten feet when he caught a glimpse of Mickey Dan. The man lay face down in the shallows of the river. Even as Scott saw him, Mickey Dan made a feeble effort to drag himself higher on the rocky beach, but the boiling current tore at him, dragging him back in. At the same time a bullet chipped granite out of a boulder ten feet from him.

Scott lay there for a moment. Afterward there was no clear thought in his brain. A man didn't think at a time like that. He simply had his impulses, and he answered them.

He rolled over till he came to a rail and then he kept

rolling, right over the top. He almost rolled off the edge and caught himself just in time. The Indians on the rim of the gorge began searching him out with their fire. With slugs driving into the ties and screaming off the rails all about him, he lowered himself down, hung to his full length, and swung like a pendulum into the trusses below. He heard Quinn's voice screaming over the din of battle.

"Scott, are ye crazy? Git back up here! They'll cut ye down, man, they'll have ye six ways from Sunday . . . !"

He couldn't answer. Deep in the maze of trusses he was pretty well covered from the fire of those Indians on the edge of the cañon.

Mickey Dan was still fighting the pull of the water, but he was pitifully weak, and it was a losing fight. The current had dragged him down under the ledge of an outcropping boulder that partially protected him from the gunfire from above. But it was pulling him on downstream, and his legs were already exposed again.

Scott saw his soggy brogan jerk as a slug hit it. The man made a feeble effort to cling to the rocks, but his fingers gradually slid off the wet granite, losing their grip entirely. His face went under water and he tried to flop over. His body thrashed feebly with the panic of a drowning man. Only a few precious moments were left. If the Indians didn't get him, the river would.

Scott dropped off the last cross-brace onto a rocky shore. Mickey Dan lay thirty feet from the protection of the bridge, and Scott would be exposed every foot of the way. He could not see Quinn from here. With a last prayer that the man would cover him, he plunged into the open. Five feet. Ten feet. The first crash of guns. The bullets slamming into the sand, ricocheting off the rocks, chipping granite into his face and drawing blood. Twenty feet. More crashing of guns, from Quinn's side this time. Mickey Dan had been dragged halfway out from the boulder now.

Scott threw himself flat beneath the overhanging boulder and pawed at the man. One hand caught the bloody shirt and the other twined in the curly black hair, pulling the head up out of the water.

Mickey Dan coughed weakly, retched. He was half drowned and unable to speak, but he saw Scott, and surprise showed feebly in his eyes. Panting, jerking spasmodically whenever a bullet came too close, Scott worked to drag the man back into cover.

But there was no cover. Fire from a new direction chipped granite off into Scott's face and made him look up the gorge. A dozen half-naked warriors were working their way down into the cañon from the rim. Their objective was apparently to cross the cañon and flank the main body of railroaders. But Mickey Dan and Scott were right in their path.

The big Irishman tried to pull himself up against the rock, reaching again, face slack and white. "Git out," he said. "They got us in a crossfire. It's just a matter o' time."

"Can you move?"

Mickey Dan shook his head. "Weak as a kitten.

Can't make anythin' work right. The world's spinnin'. Can't even see ye. How c'd a little hole in the shoulder do that?"

Scott knew it was the shock of the fall and loss of blood. He couldn't drag the man bodily back to the bridge. It wouldn't help anyway, with those warriors coming through the gorge. A moment of panic swept him as he realized how they were trapped. Then he heard a call, thin and distant, from above.

"Scott . . . Scott, me lad . . . !"

He looked up. Something was flashing in the sun. It bounded down the side of the defile. In the last instant he saw that it was a rifle and dived into the open, throwing his body across the path of its descent. The weapon struck him with a painful *thud* and he hugged it to him like a baby. Something else was coming down—the leather shoulder cases containing cartridge tubes.

One struck a rock, bounded over him, and fell into the river. He flailed an arm out, hooking it into the strap of the second as it tumbled by.

"Scott!" It was Mickey Dan's voice. "They're comin'."

He turned and saw that half a dozen of the braves had reached the broiling creek, leaping across it on a series of rocks that formed a natural dam. The first trio to reach the near side was not yet aware that Scott had a rifle and rushed to the boulder, howling and shooting.

As Scott sprawled on the rocky shore, their bullets

spewing all about him, he heard the call of a bugle run like a thin and brazen thread through all of the other din. He was dimly aware of an Indian on the bluff, standing up and shouting to those below. At the same time the others on the heights quit their cover and ran for their horses. But that trio on the near bank had not heard. Their own yells blotting out the bugle, they scrambled through the rocks at a dead run, firing as they came. The rest of it was all a howling, crashing madness, whirling around Scott like a blinding kaleidoscope of sound and movement, without coherence, without focus, without sanity.

Through it all he lay sprawled on the sand, squeezing off his shots as methodically as a sharpshooter at the firing pits, possessed of a frozen calm that could come only to a man who had gone through the same hellfire a thousand times before. Atlanta. Kennesaw Mountain. Columbia.

His front sight was covered by a coppery body and he squeezed the trigger. He saw the ruddy shape spread-eagled against the sky, and then it pitched head first into the water.

He swung to cover another running man. One of the bullets flung sand into his face, blinding him. He squeezed his trigger and heard the man's howls end in a sick grunt of pain and felt the ground tremble to his falling. He still couldn't see, but he could hear the third brave's slugs kicking up grit and granite all around him, and he swung his Spencer blindly toward the sound of his yelling and fired on an arc.

Five bullets, as fast as he could squeeze them out of the rifle, deafened him with the thunder of their passage. When the last crashing echo had died, there was no more lead kicking up the sand and no more yelling. He wiped the grit from his stinging eyes and had a watery impression of the two copper bodies sprawled in the rocks. The last one was only ten feet from him, still twitching.

Mickey Dan stared at it with wide eyes. Then he shook his head feebly. "Now I know y'r not from Connacht," he said. "Only a Galway man could shoot like that."

Chapter Nine

As soon as the Indians were gone, a dozen railroaders were clambering into the gorge to help Scott and Mickey Dan. When they reached the top of the bluff, the rest of the crew crowded around them, clapping Scott on the back and offering him a puff on their corncob pipes to steady his nerves or a nip of porter snitched from the kitchen car. Penny Quinn pushed her way into the center, taking over like a clucking hen with a lost chick. The wound in Mickey Dan's shoulder was not too serious and he was already recovering from the shock of the fall. He sat on an empty keg, smoking a fresh cigar and joking with the crew while Penny washed the wound and bandaged the arm and mothered him outrageously. The big Irishman tried to seem unconcerned, but Scott could see his eyes following Penny's every motion, her nearness bringing a flush to his face, an excited glow to his eyes.

Lieutenant Lawler rode into the group, wiping the dust from his face. "They're gone. I think that'll be all for a while."

"What were they?" Scott asked.

"Looked like Arapahoes," Lawler said.

"They didn't stay around long after you came."

"It's hit and run with them," the lieutenant answered. "They'll be back again. It only took me a few minutes to realize the attack on the train was just a diversion. There weren't over a dozen in that party."

Scott looked off into the hazy distance. "Can't blame the poor devils. We've been taking their land from them for a hundred years. This railroad will be the last step. The settlers are already flooding in. They must sense what it means."

Sean Quinn spat. "Let us all shed a tear."

Scott glanced sharply at him. "When do the English march into Dublin?"

Quinn started to squeal. Then he subsided. He pulled uncomfortably at his scraggly red beard. "I suppose y'r right. Ye can't blame the poor divils."

In five minutes the rails were going down on the bridge again, with a squad of cavalry on either side of the chasm and a dozen Spencers on the handcar. They drove the tracks half a mile beyond the bridge before dark stopped them. Then it was dinner call and the rush of men for the kitchen cars. Mickey Dan ate with them, hardly seeming the worse for wear. After dinner a dozen of them got up a game of horseshoes by the firelight and another group gathered around Quinn while he read to them out of the *Frontier Index*, the ubiquitous paper that had followed the tracks, published from boxcars and sidings, terminal towns, and tie camps. Scott paid little heed for a while, then Quinn began an article that shocked him into attention.

" 'Laramie City, May Fourteenth, Eighteen Sixty-Eight. The investigation of the Riordan murder has turned up no new evidence. Hi Bannack is recovering from his wound and apparently his explanation will stand as the final word on the whole affair. The Walkers had become enraged over the mistaken conception that they had lost their land to the railroad and came to town primed for bear. Unfortunately Mister Riordan turned out to be the bear. The Walker Gang was reportedly last seen at Fort Laramie. . . .' "

Quinn went on to another article. His voice seemed blotted out by the tumultuous rush of emotions through Scott. The exhausting labor and violence of the day had left him little time to dwell on Jade and the others. Now the thought of them took poignant focus. Fort Laramie. That was northeast, away up on the Platte. Had they been driven northeast by the pressure of pursuit? He wanted to believe that.

Either way, they were twice as far away from Rawlins Springs as he. It would give him ample time to get his horse and reach the Springs ahead of them.

For a moment he knew intense encouragement.

Then the old questions began to pound at him. What if they did all reach the Springs safely? They were still fugitives. Jade was still Noah's. What good would it do to get together again? It would only bring back the tensions, the clashes, the bitter unhappiness. Maybe she had wanted it this way. Maybe she had let them head away from Rawlins Springs deliberately, deciding that for the good of all concerned it was best that they didn't find Scott again.

He rose, and paced restlessly away from the fires. Running away from each other wasn't the answer. Jade must realize that. He had to give her the benefit of the doubt. He kept remembering the passion he had touched in her when he had first seen her in the log house. A woman didn't love one man and show another that kind of hunger. He had to see her again. They had to meet again and find the answer once and for all. They would be at Rawlins Springs if they could possibly get there. He had to believe in that.

He realized he had wandered close to the sleeping cars. Not ten feet away Penny was leaning against one of the great iron wheels, a dim shape in the darkness. She had seen him coming but half her attention was upon Mickey Dan, sitting on another upended keg, making flamboyant gestures with his cigar and giving a disgusted commentary on the quality of the horse-shoe pitchers. There was enough reflected light to show Scott the shine in Penny's eyes as she watched the Irishman.

"Your man?" Scott asked.

Her chin came up and all her attention swung to him. "Niver in a million years. Fightin' all the time, drunk half the week, every bob of his wages spent an hour after he gits 'em." Her voice was vehement.

"Maybe a woman could change that."

"Let another woman try. 'Tis not for me."

He was beside her now. The top of her tousled head hardly came to his chest. Five feet tall, curved like a milkmaid as if to make up for the lack in height, round bosom and a tiny waist and hips that filled the wool skirt as full as they filled a man's eyes. A woman made for pinching and teasing, laughter and love.

"Ever been to Cork?" he asked.

"No."

"Athlone?"

"No."

"Galway?"

"No."

"What kind of an Irishman are you?"

She smiled and leaned back. "More railroader than Irish, Mister Scott. Born in Illinois, when the Quinn was layin' tracks fer the Galena and Chicago. Got me schoolin' in a gradin' camp while we was workin' the Baltimore and Ohio. Saw me mother killed in a biler explosion while the Quinn was puttin' down rails fer the Marietta and Cincinnati."

"But this blarney," he said. "This brogue. . . ."

She nodded at the men about the campfires. "How else w'd ye talk, livin' among the likes o' them all y'r life?"

"And you mean to go on like this? The only woman in five thousand men . . . ?"

"The Quinn wouldn't know what t'do without me," she said defiantly. Then she settled back, her voice softening. "No, I don't mean t'go on. The Quinn's gittin' old. He'd go on layin' tracks till he's a hundred, but the railroad won't have it. This is the last road he'll put down, and we been lookin' around. There's a spot ahead of us on the Green River. A friend of ours is already speculatin' on a town site there. Garrett Collins. He says they're goin' to make it a division point on the U.P. A town there, and yards where a man like the Quinn could git a soft berth. A beautiful cliff above the river where ye could build a little house and hear the trains comin' through all the night long."

The nostalgia of it touched him. "That's the kind of house I'd want to visit," he said.

"Y'r welcome any time, and ye know it."

"Even if I pull down the wash?"

She chuckled. "Aye. Even so."

There was a rich current of life to this girl, a wholesomeness that seemed to shine like a beacon at the end of the dark and twisted trail he had traveled this last week. He found himself responding to it, wanting to share her sure judgment of life, her certain values, her clear vision of the road ahead. Why couldn't it have been this way with Jade?

"That was a brave thing ye did this afternoon," Penny murmured. She was watching him with half-closed eyes. "Ye've won their hearts with it."

106

"I'm glad," he said.

"And yet ye didn't like it."

He looked into the darkness. "It's something that comes to me often. I don't even know how many men I've killed. And I never knew one of them. Not one."

A shadow came to her face. "Life's a big thing. We don't get all the answers." He was silent, and after a moment she asked: "Ye were in the war?"

"Too long."

"Is that what gives ye the trouble?"

"Trouble?"

"It's in y'r eyes. Y've got somethin' that hurts, Mister Scott." She paused, then asked softly: "A woman?"

He hesitated. "Yes," he said. "A woman."

Her blue eyes snapped with mischief. "Then y've no right t'be lookin' that way at me."

He realized how close they had drawn. He moved away, smiling ruefully. "You're like sunshine, Penny. All things turn naturally to the sun."

She pouted and seemed about to answer, when the sound of voices raised in dispute drew their attention. Mickey Dan was standing by his upturned keg, bent forward, speaking with the cigar in his mouth.

"Beggin' y'r pardon, Con Dempsey," he said, "but there was ten of 'em, all runnin' and yowlin' and firin' their rifles. Cool as a cucumber he picked 'em off. Lyin' there with their bullets splatterin' the bejabbers outta the rocks all about him, frozen as ice he was. . . ."

"Excuse me," Con Dempsey said. He was a man as

107

big as Mickey Dan, black-bearded and earth-grimed, with a blacksmith's muscles bulging at his shirt and a Gaelic devil dancing in his eyes. "Excuse me, Mickey Dan, but I only saw two. . . ."

"Beggin' your pardon, Con Dempsey, the rest was pitched off inter the river, all twelve of 'em, one after the other. . . ."

"Excuse me, but how could a man with a seven-shot gun shoot twelve . . . ?"

"Beggin' y'r pardon," Mickey Dan said. He took the frayed cigar from his mouth and dropped it carefully to the earth. Then he got a fresh stogie from his pocket and bent over a fire to light it. Everybody started shouting at once, and Sean Quinn threw down his *Frontier Index*.

" 'Tis enough I've seen," he bawled. "T'the sleepin' car with ye, Mickey Dan. Y'r in no shape t'start any sich Donnybrook as this."

"Best shape o' me life," Mickey Dan said, turning back toward Con Dempsey. The other man backed away, holding up his hands, calling: "I won't have nothing t'do with it! Y'r a wounded man. Liar or not, y'r a wounded man, and I can't lay a hand on ye."

Penny made a soft little sound and started running toward them. As Scott followed her, Sean Quinn and half a dozen others surrounded Mickey Dan and tried to pull him back. He struggled mightily, roaring: "I'm a liar, now. Me, Mickey Dan, the soul o' verity, the original source o' rectitude. He's callin' me a liar and castin' aspersions on the very man that saved me life, blackenin' the sainted name of himself that was willin' to sacrifice his own noble soul to save me misbegotten hide. . . ."

Before Penny could reach them, Mickey Dan tore free of the others and lurched at Con Dempsey, shouting: "Fourteen redskins!"

"Ye said twelve before. . . ."

"Fourteen!"

"Two!"

Con Dempsey was lifted off his feet by a roundhouse blow that deposited him his full length away from Mickey Dan. He rolled over, shook his head, and scrambled erect. There was a wild look on his face and before the rest of the crowd could stop them the fight was under way.

When it was evident that Mickey Dan could hold his own despite his wound, they formed a circle around the two men and let them have at it. Penny stood squealing and moaning, holding her hands over her face and peeking through her fingers.

It was a memorable fight—titanic clouting and giant pounding and deafening shouting and blows that shook the very earth. When it was over, Con Dempsey lay stretched out unconscious on the ground and Mickey Dan stood swaying above him, dripping sweat, the cigar still glowing between his teeth.

Penny was the first to rush to him. "Ye've opened y'r wound ag'in."

He looked down at his blood-soaked shirt, grinning. "What's a good fight without a little blood?" He saw

Scott and brushed her aside. He weaved like a drunk, walking to Scott, and threw his arm across his shoulder. "Y'r reputation remains unblemished now. 'Tis a thing o' record. Fifteen redskins, cool as a cucumber."

The rest of them gathered around, laughing and joking and clouting Mickey Dan and Scott affectionately on the back. It convinced Scott that he was one of them now, that he belonged. Ever since the war he had been groping to regain this identity with the goodness of the earth, with comradeship, with laughter. This was his first real taste of it, and he drank deeply, joining in all the good-natured raillery. With his arm still over Scott's shoulder, Mickey Dan surveyed Con Dempsey. They had thrown water on the man and he was reviving slowly.

" 'Tis a good thing ye saved me life, and I can't fight ye," Mickey Dan told Scott. "I'd hate t'have it still hangin' over our heads, and me knowin' I'd have t'beat the bejabbers outta ye like that."

Scott grinned wryly. "I don't know."

"What?"

"All you know are roundhouses and haymakers," Scott said.

"And any one of 'em good enough to put a man away."

"He never touched your gut. If a man really worked your breadbasket over with a few straight jabs. . . ."

Mickey Dan withdrew his arms and backed up. He pounded himself in the belly. "Go ahead. Hard as ye can."

Scott eyed the belly, bulging a little over his belt. "Pretty soft, Mickey. Been going heavy on that porter."

Mickey Dan pounded himself again, bellowing: "I c'd stop a Baldwin locomotive! Go ahead. Straight jabs ye said. Go ahead. . . ."

He trailed off, a strange look coming to his face, because Scott hit him, hard. His mouth went slack and his eyes rolled up in his head till only the whites showed. Without a sound he pitched backward his full length. Penny went to her knees beside him with a little cry. Sean Quinn gazed down at the unconscious man, snapping his galluses thoughtfully.

"Y'r right," he said. "He is a little soft about the gut."

CHAPTER TEN

For the rest of that week Scott worked with them, and all the time, at the back of his mind, was the thought of Jade. Saturday was pay day and Scott drew twelve-fifty for five days' work. After dinner he went over to the corrals and bargained with one of the company hunters for a horse, and finally settled on a split-ear Indian pony so beefsteaked from a packsaddle that the hunter thought it useless for riding. He gave the man ten dollars and got a can of bacon grease from the cook, mixed it with gunpowder, and rubbed it into the raw patches. It was an old trapper's remedy he had learned in Montana.

111

He heard that Lawler's troop had discarded one of their McClellan saddles and he spent an hour hunting for it in the dump. The tree was broken and both stirrups had been torn off. He turned up some rawhide, stripped off the housing, and lashed the broken tree. Then he chopped up a castoff single-tree and used the wood and the remaining rawhide to fashion some makeshift stirrups. It was all a pretty sad affair but his sense of urgency was like a pressure building up in him and he couldn't wait any longer.

The next morning he paid the cook fifty cents for his breakfast and with the remaining money bought a sack of flour, a side of bacon, Triple X coffee, and a battered canteen of porter. Then he sought out Sean Quinn. The man was seated on one of the upturned kegs by the breakfast fires, like a king on his throne, surrounded by his courtiers. In their midst stood a black-haired man, gaunt and bedraggled, wearing a pair of ragged buckskins and a shirt made from a Hudson four-pointer.

"I'll have t'know a few things before I hire ye," Quinn said.

The man looked blank. *"No sabe."*

"Have ye ever been t'Athlone?"

"No hablo inglés, señor."

Quinn cocked his head. "It does have a touch o' the Gaelic to it."

"Arragh," Con Dempsey said. "He's no Irishman."

"He's got t'be!" Quinn stood up, his voice rising to cracked crescendo. "This road is bein' built by the

Irish and I'll hire no other." He waved a freckled arm at the newcomer. "Now git the cook t'feed ye and then find y'rself a sledge." Quinn saw Scott and shook his head. "*Whoosh*. What a sorry-lookin' nag."

"I'm leaving," Scott said.

There was a long silence. Finally Quinn sighed dismally. "An' here I thought y'd got the makin's of a railroader."

Mickey Dan's left arm was in a sling. He punched Scott affectionately in the shoulder with his other hand. "I understand. A Galway man's a wanderin' man. Jist see that ye cross a set o' tracks once in a while. Sooner or later ye'll meet us ag'in."

"Well," he said awkwardly. "Good bye. And thanks."

"Thanks, hell." Quinn spat. "Ye gave more than ye got."

Then Scott swung aboard the horse and rode out of their circle. He stopped by the Quinns' car. It was a flat with a cabin built on one end shared by the old man and his daughter. He wanted to say good bye to Penny, but before he could call her name she stepped into the door. She held a rolled blanket and a rusty old coffee pot in her hand.

"Ye'll need these," she said.

He heeled the horse over to her.

"I thought maybe pay day would see ye goin'," she said.

There was a shadowed sadness to her face and her eyes were soft and shining. He had the sense of something vague and amorphous between them, something begun, something that could have been. But then he thought of Mickey Dan, and the look in her eyes when she watched him. He was imagining things that weren't there.

"I hate to say good bye," he said.

"But ye have to. I know how it is, Mister Scott."

"Do one thing before I go."

"Yes."

"Drop the mister."

A smile touched her lips. "Good bye . . . Scott."

It took three days to get to Rawlins Springs through broken hills pocked with prairie-dog holes, through vast sage flats and rising broken country, across the Medicine Bow River and the North Platte. Scott watched constantly for Indian sign on the ground and kept to the ridges, careful not to skylight himself. It was a tense, nervous, exhausting ride on a horse without spirit or life.

The Springs lay on the high plains. There was a camp by the Springs, a few sod houses built by the surveying crew the year before. The only men in evidence were a pair of hunters, living in one of the sod houses. They'd been without coffee and bread for weeks and Scott shared the last of his flour and Triple X with them. Over the meal, he questioned them. They had been in advance of the railroad for months and he didn't think there was much danger of their knowing about Riordan's killing in Laramie. One was named Rapp, a lean, snuff-brown man in greasy elk-hides and beaded Ute moccasins.

"We been here a couple of weeks, waitin' for them graders," he said. "A few speculators passed through, headin' for Green River."

"I'm looking for a family," Scott said. "Two young men, a woman, an older man with white hair roached like a Missouri mule."

Rapp pulled a willow-stem pipe from a beaded holder, nodding. "A few days ago. Only stayed a few hours. Camped on the other side of the Springs. The old man and the kid was for staying here. The woman wanted to go. She kept at 'em till they took off."

Scott sank back, a sick premonition creeping through him. "They didn't leave any word?"

Rapp tamped kinnikinic into his pipe. "Not with me, they didn't."

It was like ashes in Scott's mouth. It was like the world spinning out from under him. Yankee and Feather had wanted to stay and wait for him. But Jade had wanted to go. Now he had to admit it. She had made the decision for both of them. If they had only waited a day or so, he might still know hope. But there was no other explanation. Once and for all, she had chosen Noah.

"This kinnikinic bother you?"

Scott glanced sharply at Rapp. Then he shook his head. "No."

Rapp took a long drag. "Well, you had a funny look on your face," he said.

• • •

Scott stayed with Rapp and his partner for a few days. A hundred times he went over it in his mind. A hundred times he fought his impulse to follow them, to try to find them again. It would be futile. Jade had chosen Noah and he had no right to goad her further. His presence among them, under any circumstances, would result only in the clashes again, the antagonism, the bitterness. The best thing he could do, for all concerned, was to let them alone, try to forget her, try to establish a new life for himself somewhere.

For a while he actually considered returning to the track layers. But that was changed by the arrival of the first grading crews with the news that the surveyor general was moving his headquarters west with the rails, and Hi Bannack would soon be in Rawlins Springs.

That brought it home to Scott. He was a fugitive and had to plan accordingly. The West was big. A man could lose himself somewhere in it. A man couldn't travel through the wilderness with nothing but a six-shooter, so he signed on with the graders to make enough money to buy a rifle from Rapp and to get some supplies from the commissary. Then he left Rawlins Springs.

Scott crossed the vast plain between Rawlins Spring and the Continental Divide, then on through a land of torrential rains and long, dry seasons. He reached Point of Rocks where a thousand-foot cliff towered over sulphur springs and charred surveyors' stakes marked the route of the oncoming rails.

He found a horse runners' camp there and spent some time with them trapping the wild ones. They told him the railroad would open the Jackson Hole area and there would be a big demand for stock horses as soon as the cattle outfits moved in. He thought of traveling north with the runners and establishing a stock ranch with them. But when it came time to go, he couldn't give them a final answer and they left without him.

He knew why that was. He knew what lay in him like a wound that only time would heal, leaving him without any will to make a decision or to settle down. All he could do was drift till that healing took place. Maybe then he could see his way clear.

In September he came to Green River. The town lay on the north bank of the river from which it had taken its name. It had been established by speculators, waiting for the railroad. The new buildings, most of them not yet painted, the dusty streets, the gaudy line of gingerbread façades fronting the saloons—all reminded Scott too much of Laramie.

He halted on the outskirts, filled with the impulse to skirt the town. But he was out of grub again and his clothes were threadbare and his horse needed feed and a rest. Desert dust chalked his angular face and shimmered on the shaggy edges of his untrimmed hair. He wasn't aware of it, but the primitive life he had lived these last few months and the consciousness of always running before Bannack's shadowy threat had planted little crevices of wariness at the tips of his eyes and his long lips.

He had gone a block into Green River when a sign on one side of the street caught his eye:

GREEN RIVER REALTY
GARRETT COLLINS, PROP.

He remembered Penny speaking that name. If the man was a friend of the Quinnses, perhaps he would be willing to give Scott a line on a job. Scott racked his hipshot split-ear at the hitch rail before the single-story building of peeled pine logs, its barn sash windows filmed with dust. He left his Sharps rifle in its rawhide saddle boot on the horse and went in through the open door.

His eyes found the man in the dusky interior of the office, a stocky, ruddy-faced man with a baldpate tanned deeply by the sun. He was sitting with his boots crossed on a scarred desk, studying a map in his lap. When he saw Scott, he dropped his feet off the desk and hurriedly shoved the map back among the other papers.

"Come in, sir," he said, jumping to his feet. "Glad to have you with us. Green River'll boom, oh, yes, it'll boom, you just stay around and watch. Make Rawlins Springs look like a whistle stop. Take the capital away from Laramie. Got a fine parcel of land up on the Palisades, if you're looking for a home site. No? Business place, maybe."

"I'm not in the market for that. Scott's the name. I worked for Sean Quinn on the railroad. Penny mentioned your name."

"Ah?" Collins settled back, his eyes beginning to twinkle. "Penny," he said reminiscently. "How is the little firebrand?"

"Still running the U.P.," Scott said.

Collins stood quickly and pulled out a chair. "Sit down, Scott. Any friend of Sean's is a friend of mine. I've got some mighty fine peach somewhere here." He pulled out drawers, ruffled through papers and briefcases, finally uncovering a bottle. Without sitting down, Scott said: "Before I take so much hospitality, maybe I better tell you. I need a job."

Collins chuckled. "Plenty here for a hard worker. Can you blacksmith?"

"Fair enough."

"You're set, then." Collins poured a drink and offered it to him. "Those graders'll be here soon. A hundred teams to need shoeing. Never have enough o' their own smiths for the work. Our stables will be busy twenty-four hours a. . . ."

Still holding the drink out to Scott, he stopped. A fugitive apprehension passed through his face. He was looking beyond Scott, and his mouth was open. There was the hollow *clatter* of boots from behind him and Scott wheeled quickly. Two men were entering the door.

One was tall and lanky, moving with a shambling stride. Perhaps it was a trick of light. His eyes seemed to have no depth behind their half-drawn lids. He wore greasy elk-hide leggings, indented around his right thigh by the rawhide thong holding his gun down.

Behind him came a shorter man, immensely broad through the shoulders, with a wide waist that had a singular girth without giving the sense of fatness. He moved like a man keeping his balance on a tight wire. His face was broad and battered, one ear smashed to unrecognizable pulp against his head, livid little scars mottling his cheek bones. "Afternoon, Mister Collins," he murmured. "Come to clean up our little deal."

There was a pause, and then Collins said: "Aren't you jumping the gun, Taw? I haven't got any deed yet."

Taw shook his head. "The deed won't be released till the lease is signed. You've got to show good faith." He indicated the other man. "Ed Cabinet wants to start cutting his ties as soon as possible. If you'll make out the papers, we can start the wheels rolling."

Irritation compressed Collins's lips. "You're really pushing things, aren't you?"

Taw's battered face went blank for a moment. Then his lips spread in a grin that almost closed his eyes. "Why shouldn't we? The deal's all set up. You made it a long time ago."

"I can't lease something I don't own."

"You own it. The papers are on their way. But the land company won't release anything at this end till they see that lease. It's all contingent, Collins. I explained before."

"Not quite clearly enough."

"You mean you're backing out of the deal?"

"Don't twist things up. I merely want everything to be in order."

Ed Cabinet's moccasins made a sibilant stir against the floor. "I thought all the talking was over with," he said.

"It is," said Taw. "Mister Collins is going to sign the papers and we're going to give him the money and the deal will be closed."

An old man's irascible anger pinched in Collins's cheeks. "Damn you, Taw! Don't try to pull anything phony on me. I won't sign anything till it's time. Why don't you come back later? I've got a customer."

Taw turned to Scott with that grin fixed on his face. "Your customer can come back later."

A corner of Scott's attention caught up the expression in Collins's face. The man's eyes fluttered and grew luminous with what was almost a plea. His cheeks seemed to have sucked in, creating strained hollows at the tips of his mouth. Scott had seen enough men in fear during these last months to read it in Collins. He felt his weight settle forward slightly onto the balls of his feet and met Taw's meaningless smile with one as fixed and humorless.

"I'd be glad to go if I thought you had business here," he said.

"That's right," Collins said. "Now, please, Taw, do as I ask. We can talk later."

"There isn't anything to talk about," answered Taw.

He walked to the desk, pulling papers from his coat, laying them down. "There are the papers. Sign them. The money's in my wallet."

"No." Collins's cheeks seemed to pinch in farther, and he shook his head jerkily. "Not now, Taw. . . ."

"Now!" As he said it, Taw's thick arm lashed upward with surprising speed, catching the front of Collins's coat and hauling him forward. "Are you going to sign, Collins," asked Taw, "or are you going to get hurt?"

"Let the man go," Scott told him.

Without turning toward him, Taw said: "Get him out of here, Cabinet. . . ."

But Scott had expected this. He was already lunging for Cabinet as the man reacted. Scott reached the man before he had his gun free. The impact pinned Cabinet against the wall, too stunned to go on drawing his weapon. It gave Scott time to step back and then forward again, putting all his weight in the blow at Cabinet's belly. The loose-jointed man jackknifed with a gusty sound. He hung there a last moment, doubled over with agony, then pitched helplessly to the floor.

Taw let go of Collins to whirl for Scott, his right hand dipping under the lapel of his coat. Scott lunged for Taw. The man did not have his gun free as Scott went into him, deliberately pinning that right arm up between them. Scott let him have it in the belly with his own right.

It was like hitting a pig of Galena lead. Taw grunted, his heavy body smashing back into the desk. He twisted a shoulder into Scott so he could pull his right arm free without the gun in time to block Scott's next blow. Then his whole thick body twisted back the other way, throwing all its weight skillfully into the punch of his left hand at Scott's face.

It rocked Scott's head back. It would have knocked him away if he hadn't caught the man's arm. Taw tried to tear free, but Scott pulled him off balance and swung him around, yanking that arm up into a hammerlock. It went halfway up the man's back, and then stopped.

Scott shouldered in under, applying more leverage. But the arm would not move. Sweat broke out on his face as he added the peak of his own strength to the leverage. Still the arm would not move. It was a hold few men could block. In any other circumstances he could have jerked the arm up and torn it free of the socket. It made him realize, for the first time, what an incredible strength laid in this massive man.

For that moment they were stalemated, straining in a static pose. Cabinet was making retching noises on the floor and trying to get up. Collins had jumped back against the wall, staring open-mouthed at Scott.

"Don't try to wrestle him, you fool," he gasped.

The sweat beaded Taw's face as he began to force that arm straight again. Slowly, inexorably, it came down. Another moment and Taw would be able to turn about on Scott.

Scott let go suddenly. The man spun toward Scott with the violence of his own reaction. Scott kicked one of his feet from beneath him, hitting the man in the face with all his weight. The blow caught Taw off balance and carried him up and over the top of the desk, and he fell heavily to the floor. Dazedly he tried to roll over and pull his gun again. Scott followed him across the desk and jumped down at the man, kicking the gun from his hand with a vicious lash of one boot. It skittered across the floor into the wall.

"Scott," cried Collins, "look out!"

Scott heard the rustling sound from the other side of the desk and wheeled to see Cabinet up on his knees, still bent over, his right hand on his gun.

"Go ahead," Scott said, "if you aren't satisfied with a lickin'."

Cabinet looked at the gun at Scott's hip. A dull defeat flickered in his eyes. Cabinet pulled his hand off his gun, and got painfully to his feet. Taw was rising, too, hugging his kicked hand under his opposite arm, pain forming squinted grooves at the corners of his eyes. Then that grin began to spread. It had about as much humor now as a naked blade.

"You're new in town."

"That's right," Scott told him.

"You got a lot to learn."

"When does school open?"

Taw licked his lips maliciously. "I'll let you worry about that."

He turned to pick up his gun, but Scott's voice stopped that. "Never mind. Collins can ship it back to you sometime."

Taw paused. Then a dogged expression settled into the battered features. He shrugged and turned to walk around the desk, jerking his head for Cabinet to follow him out. The sounds of fighting had already gathered a crowd and it blocked up the door. Taw stopped there, raking the bystanders with his eyes. Scott saw the fearful subservience in the faces of half a dozen men as they gave way swiftly for his passage. After he was gone, they closed up and began to press into the office. Collins was by the desk, brushing himself off.

"What happened, Garrett?" asked a potbellied man. "Taw try to give you a going over?"

"They would have if Scott here hadn't stopped them," said Collins.

A towheaded man in bib overalls stared owlishly at Scott. "You ain't pulling our leg?"

"You saw them leave, didn't you, Simms?" Collins told him, grinning now. He jerked his head toward the gun lying on the floor. "Took Taw's gun away from him, too, and never even pulled his own. You've been looking for a town tamer, gentlemen. What do you think of this man for our marshal?"

"A stranger?" Simms asked.

"Ain't no stranger now, Simms," Collins said. He moved over to clap Scott affectionately on the shoulder. "He's met half a dozen of the town's leading citizens, made a lifelong friend of the biggest land speculator west of the Missouri, lifelong enemies of the two most dangerous men in our little municipality.

Most of you folks have been here for weeks without accomplishing that much."

The potbellied man tugged at his snakeskin galluses, frowning at Scott. "But we don't even know who he is."

"He's already presented us with his references, Morse," Collins said. "Honesty? What's more honest than defending a stranger just because you think he's right. Courage? Which one of you is willing to stand up against Taw and Cabinet single-handed? Efficiency? Disarming two of the most lethal characters in Green River without even pulling his gun?"

"We haven't even asked the man himself," Simms said.

Collins gaped at the man. Then he looked at Scott, grinning sheepishly. "You wanted a job, didn't you?"

"I did," admitted Scott. "But I didn't have anything like this in mind."

"The best you could do shoeing horses is maybe forty dollars a month," Collins said. "Our marshal gets three hundred a month during peacetime and ten dollars a day bonus while the railroad is passing through. We need a man like you, son. Our mayor and trustees are elected. The territorial legislature's going to give us a charter. All that's left is to elect our officers of the law." He wheeled on the others. "And we can't delay much longer. Those graders will be reaching us soon. Five hundred drunken Irishmen in here every Saturday night, gentlemen. I saw what it did to Kearney and Julesburg. If you want anything left of your town, you'd better have your law enforcement organized."

A murmur ran through the group and Morse thumbed his galluses thoughtfully. "You're right, Collins. It won't hurt to talk it over. If you want to nominate this man, I'm willing to call a meeting of the trustees."

"Consider him nominated," Collins said.

Scott's reaction was one of indifference, of reckless-ness. He knew the danger involved. He had seen the violence of Laramie. It wasn't just an ordinary law officer's job. He also needed the money. He had known how foolish he was, clinging to the terminal towns, with the possibility of meeting somebody from Laramie, or of Bannack catching up with him, but a man needed more than a jaded horse and a gun to cut free of these lonely points in civilization and cross the wilderness stretching on every side. A week or so on a marshal's pay might do it.

"All right," he said. "I accept the nomination. But I can't do it under false pretenses. What you're mainly interested in is a man to control those railroad crews. I'll try to do that, but don't expect me to stay on after-ward."

Morse nodded. "I'll present it to the trustees that way. A marshal *pro tem*."

He turned to walk up the street and the others drifted off with him. Beaming, Collins shut the door and went around the desk. He picked the bottle of peach brandy off the floor, uptilted it. A last dribble ran out and he set the bottle on the desk with a disgusted sound.

"What's this deal you had with Taw?"

Collins wheezed, stooping to gather papers off the floor. "I'm a land speculator, Scott. There are a lot of sharks in my business, but basically it's legitimate. I made my killing at Cheyenne. Before the rails hit there, town-site lots were selling at two hundred and fifty dollars. I bought twenty of them from the Union Pacific Land Company. Six months later I sold them at thirty-five hundred dollars apiece. It's the way every town has boomed along the railroad."

"And now Green River."

"This is different," Collins said. "I'm getting along. I want to settle here. There's a chance to make it a beautiful little town, a place a man could be proud to live in."

He went to the dusty window and gestured outside. Scott could see the sandstone bluffs towering a thousand feet above the river northward from town.

"We call those the Palisades. The most beautiful part of town, the most beautiful residence section along the whole Union Pacific. To get hold of it I sank every last dollar I own."

"And then the land company tells you there's been a mistake," Scott said. "The Palisades don't really fall into the town site. They're Public Domain and are part of the twenty sections the railroad gets for every mile of track laid."

Collins was surprised. "What?"

"So Taw comes into the picture. He says there's nothing on the Palisades the railroad can use and they're willing to compromise if you'll give him a ninety-year timber lease. . . ."

Collins walked around the desk. "Did the railroad send you?"

"Something very similar happened in Laramie," Scott said. "What is Taw here?"

"The deputy surveyor."

"For the government, or the railroad?"

"Technically, neither. These deputy surveyors are private contractors, employed on a job-to-job basis by the surveyor general of the district."

"In each case they're apparently trying to get control of a piece of land," Scott said. "The timber rights aren't worth such a fuss. Is there a chance that the tracks would go through the Palisades? A surveyor would know it before anybody else. He could get possession of the land and hold out for a high price from the railroad."

"Doesn't add up," Collins said. "First, the fraud would be too obvious. Second, why should they bridge from way up there when they can cross the river on the flats?"

"How about mineral rights?"

"Hell," Collins said. "If there was anything worth mining on the land, the U.P. would know it. Look how they developed those iron beds around Rawlins Springs. They'll be getting all the red paint they need for a hundred years."

"Then what is it?"

"Damned if I can figure it out." Collins squinted at

129

him. "You say the circumstances were the same at Laramie?"

"Almost identical."

"What happened?"

"The people involved lost everything."

Collins frowned. "It sounds ugly."

Scott looked at the mild little man, thinking of Yankee, of his brothers, of Jade. He shook his head somberly. "Uglier than you can imagine, Collins."

CHAPTER ELEVEN

Collins took Scott to dinner. He wanted to stake him to the meal, but Scott made him put it on the basis of a loan against his marshal's salary. Afterward they went to the clapboard Land Office. The lamp-lit room was blue with smoke, crowded with tinhorn speculators and men buying and trading town-site lots. The clerk was the potbellied little man named Morse who Scott had met earlier. He explained the Palisades situation to Scott carefully.

His preliminary plats had placed the Palisades within the town site and he had made the sale to Collins accordingly. Before title was cleared he got a change that showed the Palisades to be in one of the alternate sections granted the railroad along their right-of-way. Collins's money was refunded. But it was only a small portion of the sum Collins had already spent in building contracts and Eastern advertising. This would be forfeited if Collins couldn't get the land.

"Where do these plats come from?" Scott asked.

"The surveyor general's office," Morse told him.

"Would they pass through Hi Bannack's hands in Laramie?"

Morse nodded. "He had somethin' to do with 'em."

"And they're based on Taw's original survey out here?"

"That's right," Morse said. "He's deputy surveyor."

"What would happen if a mistake was made in the original surveys?"

"Taw's bondsmen would have to forfeit their money."

"And that didn't happen?"

"No."

"But a mistake was made."

"Apparently a clerical error. Out of Taw's hands."

Scott thanked the man, walked outside with Collins. They stood in the warm spring evening and Scott fingered his empty shirt pocket. Collins saw it and got out his own makings and rolled two cigarettes.

"Thanks," Scott said. "You think the clerk's in on it?"

"Not Morse. He's straight as they come."

"That's what I figure," Scott said. "I don't think the railroad knows what's happening. Only one survey went in to the survey general's office. The rest of the juggling is being done somewhere along the way."

"But why? The U.P. Land Company is apparently willing to sell the land whether it falls in the town site or in one of their alternate sections."

"Would you have signed that timber lease if you didn't have to?"

Collins frowned. "Of course not."

"Maybe that's the key. They had to get you in a position where you'd sign the lease. Maybe the survey never put the Palisades in the town site at all. That was just the come-on. That first plat you saw was a phony. Then, when the switch was made, you thought you had to sign the lease to save your investment."

"But Morse never questioned the deal."

"Why should he? Everything looks straight to him. The original survey comes from Taw and the final plats pass through Bannack's hands. Between Taw out here and Bannack back there almost any switch can be pulled."

Collins shook his head. "But why? If Taw or this Bannack had wanted the land, they could have got title to it themselves."

"If you're pulling a fraud, do you put your name to it? The land would be in your name, the lease would be in Cabinet's name. On the surface, the whole thing has no connection with Taw or Bannack."

"But they must have known I would catch on sooner or later."

"Maybe that isn't as big a flaw as it seems. If you exposed them at any stage in the game, your life savings would still go down the drain. Wouldn't a man be willing to overlook a lot . . . to hang on to that?"

Collins shook his head helplessly. "Damn it!" he said.

They walked together to the realty office. In the back room were a couple of rusty beds, a cracked mirror, a crockery wash basin. They sat on the beds for an hour, smoking. Collins poked a dozen holes in Scott's hypothesis, and by the time they were finished Scott wondered how he could have been so certain about it all. Finally Collins told him he could bunk there that night and they turned in.

Scott woke before the older man next morning, dressed, and went outside to wash at the trough before Craig's General Store next door. The town was coming awake. A swamper was washing down the splintery walk in front of the Royal Flush halfway down the block and a sleepy rider passed at a trot, yawning and rubbing his eyes. From the Grader's Café issued half a dozen freighters, joking and picking their teeth.

Then Scott saw the wagon coming in off the desert—cut-under Studebaker piled high with cook stove and baggage and heaps of dirty laundry. He had once tipped that wagon over.

The same girl was driving. Then she saw him and slapped at the team with her reins, urging them into a run. She didn't stop them till she was a few feet away, putting all her weight on the reins and jamming a foot against the brake. The wagon came to a skidding, squealing stop, kicking grit all over him. He grinned up at her and she grinned down at him. Her face was flushed and she didn't try to hide the pleasure in her eyes.

Suddenly she stood up, holding out her arms, and he

133

stepped to the wagon and swung her down. She held onto his arms tightly.

"If it wasn't such broad daylight, I think I c'd hug ye," she said.

"One more day without that brogue and I think I would have died," he said.

They laughed together, and he had the fierce impulse to hold her tightly. Then the thought of Jade came to him, like a shadow between them. Perhaps Penny sensed it. She let go his arms and pulled back.

"Did ye find y'r woman?"

"That's over."

"For good?"

"For good."

"I'm sorry."

"Don't be," he said. "It's best this way."

A mischievous smile tugged at her lips. "Maybe I'm not really sorry."

Jade's shadow seemed to fade. "Are the rails this close?" he asked.

"Twenty miles," she said. "That could mean two weeks. I came ahead. There's a washerwoman I'll be livin' with here. We'll have plenty o' laundry to do till the Quinn arrives. Then he'll pick out our house with me and I'll have it ready by the time he finishes layin' the rails."

"Up on the bluffs," he said.

She turned to look at the cliffs, shimmering in the bright morning light. "Have ye seen the view from up there yet?"

Damn Taw, he thought. "No," he said. "We'll see it, together."

He woke Collins and there was a happy reunion, and then they rode with Penny to the Cassidy house in the west end of town. Gwen Cassidy was the widow of a stage driver, plump, gray-haired, motherly. They had to stay for breakfast, and Scott offered to help with the dishes but the women wouldn't have it. He sprawled in a chair and watched Penny and Mrs. Cassidy bustling in the kitchen. Collins glanced at him shrewdly.

"Good for a man," he said.

Scott didn't look at him. "You're right."

"I've proposed to Gwen a dozen times." Collins chuckled. "She says she can't see it with a land shark."

Later Collins went down to the temporary city hall to find out what the trustees had decided. Scott spent his time helping Penny sort the wash she had brought along. When they were finished, he suggested they ride up on the Palisades.

Scott took the reins and headed the Studebaker down the main street. At the edge of town a rider approached them, coming off the desert—a nervous man on a nervous horse. Sitting tall and tight-shouldered in the saddle and glancing behind him like a wolf on the run, alkali covered the man's grease-blackened buckskins like patches of snow. Desert dust had turned his face to a gaunt and chalky mask. His

135

hair, lying beneath his hat brim in a long and ragged mane, was bleached bone-white by the sun. Kalispel.

He recognized Scott and couldn't check his sudden jerk on the reins that set his pony to dancing sideways beneath him. It took him past the wagon twenty feet. His eyes were like holes burned through a blanket.

Penny looked at Scott's face. "What is it?" she asked.

"Nothing." He glanced over his shoulder. He didn't want to turn his back on the man, but Kalispel was faced toward town and had lifted his pony to a canter. "It's all right," he said.

"Ye know him?"

"Yes."

"He looked bad. I've seen his kind before."

He did not answer. There was a growing sickness in him, the helpless frustration of the fugitive. What was Kalispel doing here? Would Bannack be next? He hadn't thought it would come so soon. He had hoped he could last a week or so, had hoped he could fulfill the obligation he accepted when he took the marshal's job. He looked down at his hands. They were pale at the knuckles and trembling.

The ride up to the bluffs was silent, strained. Penny seemed to sense the intense confusion in him. She made an attempt to break the mood, but he couldn't respond. Collins had started a new cliff road although it wasn't completed and they had to take the old trail, a roundabout way up through the gullies and draws and thick scrub timber. They stopped at the edge of the bluffs and had a breathtaking view. The town was like toy houses laid out in precise squares below. To the north the river sparkled like a silver ribbon, and to the west stretched the desert, vast, illimitable, haze-ridden. Penny breathed deeply.

"Such a clean smell, off the river. And the trains whistling down there as they go through."

A place to stop, he thought. The knowledge that they were coming, that they were here, driving him away, making him run, suddenly made him want to stay, more than anything else in the world. He turned to her with the need naked in his face and she saw it, and her whole body lifted toward him as if with an impulse to reassure, to help.

It made the need change shape. It made him realize that it was this girl who had focused it all for him. The town was but a symbol and she was the reality. He put his hands to her and kissed her. It was none of the passion he had known with Jade, the straining of body to body, the fire roaring in his head. It was the sun warm on his cheek and the wind blowing down from distant peaks full of the clean smell of shadowed pools and pungent pine. Her lips were full and sweet on his, moist, velvety, yielding. His hands were on her soft round shoulders and he felt a tremor run through her body and he pulled back a few inches to look into her face.

Tears lent a silvery shimmer to the surface of her eyes and he saw confusion in her for the first time.

"Maybe I took something that wasn't mine to take," he said.

Her voice was no more than a whisper. "Ah, Scott," she said. "Scott. . . ."

"Mickey Dan?" he asked.

"He has no claim on me."

"Maybe I haven't, either."

"Don't say it." She bowed her head. She was close to crying.

"Then what is it?"

"Somethin' dark in ye. Some trouble." She raised her head, reaching to put a soft palm against his cheek. "It stands between us. I want t'help ye, but it stands there like a shadow all the time, between us."

"I told you it was over with the woman."

"And still somethin's there. Is that man part of it?"

"Kalispel?"

"Kalispel." She repeated the name. "It sounds like him. Wild and ugly."

He settled back in the seat, looking off into the distance. A rig of some sort was coming in from the east, down the road, out of the desert. Scott's eyes grew blank and the shadows lay darkly in the hollows of his angular face.

"We'd better go back," he said.

CHAPTER TWELVE

Dusk was falling when they reached Mrs. Cassidy's. She told them Collins had been there and had left word that the trustees had approved Scott's appointment as marshal. He was waiting for Scott in the real estate office now.

• Scott took his leave of Penny and walked toward the main street through the gathering night. A line of freight wagons rolled in from the east, the creaking of their wheels echoing shrilly against the false-fronted buildings. Men gathered in shadowy little knots around the doors of the saloons, the barbershop, their cigarettes winking like fireflies in the sooty darkness. Scott watched warily for the gleam of window light against that blond hair, but he saw no sign of Kalispel.

At first he had been filled with the impulse to turn down the marshal's job. He had no right to stay, to drag Penny into this. He had realized that up on the bluffs. What would happen if he left? To that land up on the Palisades, to Collins and his dream of a town, to an old railroader's dream of a spot to stop and the sound of the trains coming through during the night? The same kind of dreams had been smashed back at Laramie. Would he be exposing them to the same thing if he left? Collins. Penny. Would he really be running out on her?

A swamper brought a ladder out and began to light

the lamps in front of the T-Rail Saloon. Scott turned down an alley toward the real estate office.

A treacherous backlight of the lamps seeped into the alley, striving futilely to impregnate the thickening darkness. Scott was halfway through when a subdued *clatter* of the boardwalk came from behind him. His apprehension made him turn to look.

A man stepped off the walk, coming after him into the alley. He was blocked out against the light of the main street, a singularly broad man, the immense girth of his shoulders and torso seeming to make him top-heavy so that he rolled slightly as he walked.

Then there was the slightest stir of motion down at the other end of the alley. The motion persisted, slowly resolving itself as it came toward him, becoming the shadowy figure of another man. He had a flat-footed shamble, his movements loose-jointed, his long arms hanging like an ape's from deeply sloping shoulders.

Scott put his back up against a building, where he could keep both of them in his sight. They each approached him from about the same distance. He took a deep, steadying breath. They were within five paces of him.

"Don't come any closer," he told them. "Unless you want to start something."

They both stopped. The broad man who had entered from the street spoke. "School ain't opened yet, Walker."

Taw's voice.

140

"Yeah," the other man said. "All we want is talk."

Cabinet.

"A man wants to see you at the Royal Flush," Taw said.

"Kalispel?"

"Bannack."

Scott felt his body jam itself harder against the wall. The light from the street washed feebly against Cabinet's equine face. It made his eyes wink like silver coins. "You comin'?" he asked.

Scott tried to see his way clear. If they had wanted to get him, they wouldn't have bothered talking. Then Bannack really wanted to see him. Why?

"What can you lose?" Taw asked.

He saw some logic to it. There was really only one way he could lose, under the circumstances. And he could pretty well check that out.

"Go ahead of me," he said. "Both of you."

Cabinet walked around in front of him, his gun harness rustling mutedly. Scott watched that harness carefully until the man was past him. Then, as they both turned to walk out of the alley, he pulled his Navy Colt. He followed them into the dark street. The Royal Flush was at the west end of town, separated from the other cluster of saloons by a pair of blocks. Craig's General Store and the harness shop flanked it. Scott followed the men down an alley between the saloon and the harness shop. Lighted windows made twin yellow squares against the night-blackened wall. Taw opened a door that led into a short hall, floored with splintery planks. Another door. Taw opened it, and for the first time he turned to glance at Scott. He saw the revolver in Scott's hand. The grin broadened, completely closing his eyes.

"Go ahead," Scott said.

Taw went in. Cabinet followed. The first man Scott saw as he entered was Kalispel. He stood with his back to the rear wall, facing the door. The drumming of his fingers against one leg made a nervous little tattoo in the room. It didn't stop when he saw Scott, but a sudden flame leaped into his milky eyes, wild and vicious and a little insane.

The next step Scott took into the room brought him past the open door and revealed Bannack. The man had apparently been studying a large map of the town site and environs on the wall. He had a glass of apricot brandy in one freckled hand and its fruity scent filled the room.

The scars of the beating Yankee had given him still lay across his blunt cheek bones like chalk marks. His eyes were rusty with an old malice. He saw the gun in Scott's hand and said: "What the hell?"

Taw reached for the doorknob, and Scott said sharply: "Don't shut it."

Taw checked his motion, glanced at Bannack. The red-headed man gave no reaction. Taw settled back and the five of them stood looking at one another without speaking. Finally Bannack put down his drink.

"Not very smart," he said, "to stay in town."

142

"Did you want me to leave?"

Bannack tucked thumbs under the lapel of his handsome mauve fustian. "I was in your spot, my first impulse would be to run."

"Maybe a man gets tired of running."

"What else can he do?"

"Start asking questions, maybe."

"What questions?"

"Like why you should bother talking with me."

Bannack pursed his lips. In the lamplight his flesh looked as pale as dough and the freckles stood out boldly against his cheeks. "I want to give you a chance, Scott. We all know it was your father that killed Riordan."

"Why didn't you tell that to the *Index?*"

Bannack made an impatient gesture. "I gave them the facts. I can't be responsible if some reporter gets it garbled. The law classes you all together now. The Walker gang." He looked at Scott from beneath bushy red brows, but Scott gave no reaction. Bannack's voice grew heavier. "There's a United States marshal on the case, Scott. I understand he's at Benton now. All I'd have to do is drop the word."

"Then why don't you?"

Bannack glanced at Taw. "I told you. I wanted to give you a chance."

"Or maybe you don't want me caught."

"That's gratitude," Taw said.

"Gratitude, hell." Scott spoke to Bannack. "You expected me to run and I didn't. You're afraid if I'm caught, I'll talk. It would blow the whole lid off what you're doing here."

Bannack frowned. "And just what do you think I'm doing here?"

"The same thing you were doing at Laramie."

"I was merely carrying out my duties as deputy surveyor."

It had been guesswork up to now, but Scott saw that it had put Bannack on the defensive. The possibility that he was on the right track made Scott try a bluff. As Taw had said: what could he lose?

"We know what you were doing at Laramie," Scott said. "Do you think a man could homestead Cheyenne Parks for a year and not know what you wanted on that land?"

"Scott," Bannack said, "you don't know a damn' thing."

Scott smiled enigmatically. "Then why did you bother talking with me?"

Bannack showed anger for the first time. His jaw clamped shut and his fists closed. "The law's closer than Benton. One word in this town and you're indicted for murder."

"Checkmate, Bannack."

"What?"

"Nobody to arrest me. As of today, I'm the law in Green River."

Chapter Thirteen

Scott left the Royal Flush borne on a strange sense of triumph. He remembered his impulse to run before, his questions, his doubts. It was all gone now. He knew what he wanted to do. He wanted to stay. He had found a chink in Bannack's armor and he wanted to stay and fight it out.

He had shaken them. He didn't know a thing and he had shaken them. The next few days would be the test. If his bluff hadn't convinced them, they would undoubtedly expose him. But if they were really afraid of what he might know—afraid of his knowledge reaching the law and blowing what they had here sky-high—it was stalemate. And that was better than running. After months of being pushed by their threat behind him it gave him a sense of power to stand and fight.

He stepped out on the street and looked up at the cliffs. He remembered his need to stay here, to know all the town could give and all a woman like Penny could give. He had the chance, slim as it was, to fight for that now. But it had to be right. If it was with Penny, it had to be right.

He went back to Mrs. Cassidy's house. Penny answered the door. She invited him into the parlor and poured him a glass of tea. They sat in a pool of lamplight that burned like a subdued fire in her tumbled mass of hair. She sat with her little freckled hands folded in her lap, and her voice was a rustle in the silent room.

"Ye're an officer of the law now?"

"That depends on you," he said.

Her brows arched in surprise. He told her—about Jade, about Laramie, about Yankee and Noah and Feather, Riordan, Bannack, Cheyenne Parks. It was like a confession. When he had finished, he rose and walked to the window, his back to her.

"I want to stay, Penny," he said. "I want to fight them. But you're the one who made me want to. Without you, I think I'd have run again, without even waiting for this evening. So I couldn't lie any longer. I had to know whether you could accept me as Scott Walker or not."

She didn't answer for a while and he could hear the faint sigh of her breathing. Then she rose and came up behind him.

"I understand, Scott. And I believe what ye say. Ye're no killer. I've heard of the Walkers and I've thought of them as mean and dangerous, like a dog turned on its master. But ye're none of that. What ye're runnin' from is none o' y'r own makin' and the lies that had t'be. I think ye should stay." She paused. "I want ye to."

He wheeled to her. He took her in his arms and kissed her, and then held her. He could feel her heart thudding, and his fingers sank deeply into the satiny flesh of her back. Finally she arched back over his arms, looking into his face. Her cheeks were flushed

146

and her eyes held a jeweled sparkle.

"Ye should tell Collins," she said. "Ye can trust him."

"I planned to," he said. "I didn't want to drag him into this unless he knew the truth. I've got to give him the chance to back out."

They left a note for Mrs. Cassidy and went together to the realty office. Collins was in the back room studying his plats. Scott told him, and before he was half through Collins was pacing a circle around the splintery deal table, scratching absently at his sun-reddened pate, shaking his head. When Scott was done, Collins nodded to himself.

"Now I understand so much. So much." He looked at Penny. "You believe this?"

"Every word."

"And you want him to stay?"

"I do."

"I wanted to give you the chance to back out, as far as the marshal's job goes," Scott said. "I know it might cause you trouble if it were known you'd backed Scott Walker."

"Oh, hell!" Collins said. "If Penny believes in you, I believe in you. As far as the trustees go, it's a matter of timing. If we tell them your true identity now, they might back off. But if you prove you can handle those railroad gangs, I know they'll want you. Your reputation's really pretty pale beside some of these town-tamers. They made a professional killer marshal of Julesburg for a while. It's a rough job, Scott, and they

147

need a man who can handle it too bad to look very far into his background."

"What's your suggestion?"

"That you take the job if you want to. If Bannack exposes you, we'll meet that bridge when we come to it. If he doesn't, we'll let the trustees get a few nights with the railroad crews under their belts, then we'll tell them your true name ourselves."

Scott rose, his dark eyes kindling as he smiled at them. "It's good to have such friends," he said.

"It's what ye've needed for a long time," Penny said.

Collins led them through the dark front office to open the door for them. He pulled it part way back, and then stopped. Over his shoulder, Scott looked into the street. Shadowy shapes were going by, horsemen and a creaking Espenshied piled with freight. A man came through the door of the Tie-Camp Bar and light poured into the dark notch between the bar and the Ute Hotel next door. Like liquid stain it licked up the shape of the figure standing in the notch—the sloping shoulders, the long arms, the eyes like silver coins.

Collins shut the door. But Penny had caught a glimpse of Cabinet. She came against Scott with her fists up against his chest.

"I didn't think of that, Scott. Don't let us push ye into this."

He held her by the shoulders, searching the features of her face in the semidarkness. "I made my own choice, Penny. But you should understand it clearly. I

148

think it'll be this way from here on out. I'm dangerous to Bannack here. He'll try to get rid of me."

"And if he's afraid to have the law reach you. . . ."

She trailed off. He knew the alternative she was thinking of.

"I'm afraid, Scott. I've got to admit it. I'm afraid for ye."

"If it was you," he said, "would you run again?"

He saw her chin come up and almost felt the crackle of anger run through her. "I would not. . . ." She broke off, realizing what she was saying.

He chuckled. "I didn't think so. Now let's go out the back way."

After leaving Penny at Mrs. Cassidy's, he returned by the main street, careful not to silhouette himself against any windows, watching for Cabinet. The man was waiting for him on the corner by the T-Rail Saloon. They paralleled each other down the street, on opposite sides. Cabinet made no attempt to hide. He stopped in the notch between the Ute and the Tie-Camp and watched Scott let himself into the realty office. Scott lit the hurricane lamp. He had just finished when the front door clattered, and he wheeled, hand on his gun. Collins appeared, carrying a double-barreled Greener in the crook of one elbow.

"You!" Scott exclaimed.

"You didn't think I was going to let them blow out your lamp, did you?"

Scott chuckled and clapped him on the back. "Bannack doesn't know what a tiger he's got by the tail."

Collins snorted and put down the gun. Scott asked him for pencil and paper and then sat down at the table to make out a list. It had been going through his mind on the way back from Penny's and he had it pretty well worked out.

Expectorating on the sidewalk . . . five dollars.
Blocking traffic . . . five dollars or one day.
Breaking bottles in the streets . . . twenty dollars.
Cruelty to animals . . . ten dollars or five days.
Breaking windows . . . five dollars or one day.
Jaywalking . . . ten dollars or two days.
Lying in the street . . . fifteen dollars or five days.

Collins looked over his shoulder and made a surprised sound. "What's all this? Who's going to lie in the street?"

Scott stuck the pencil between his teeth, grinning. "Did you ever hear of blue laws, Garrett?"

"No."

"You will."

The next morning Scott met with the trustees in the temporary city hall, the big tack room at the rear of Holichek's livery. There were eight men on the board, drawn from all walks of life. Bob Morse, possessed of a sardonic humor, was chief clerk in the Land Office. Mayor Craig ran the General Store. Judge Fogarty was Justice of the Peace, the sole arbiter of the law between here and Laramie. The whole board was only

150

a provisional body, in power until the charter was granted and a regular council should be elected. Before Craig administered the oath of office, Scott stood at the head of the table and made his little speech.

"I'll be glad to accept this appointment, gentlemen, providing I can choose my own deputies and have this list of laws put on the statutes."

They gathered around and bent their heads over the sheet of paper. Craig made a disgusted sound and slapped the paper.

"Are you trying to pull our leg, Scott? What's this jaywalking?"

"Crossing the street except at intersections."

"And spitting on the walk," Morse said. "How in hell can we stop men from that?"

Judge Fogerty began to chuckle softly. "It looks like Mister Scott has gone back to our Puritan grandfathers, gentlemen. You'll find some of these statutes, silly as they seem, still on the books in some of our Eastern communities."

"Can I expect your co-operation?" Scott asked.

Judge Fogerty was still smiling. "If this is one of the protections you intend setting up against railroaders, we'll back you up. If you find a man deliberately lying in the street, you can certainly arrest him for violating one of our most fundamental statutes."

They all had to laugh, and before it died down Craig was administering the oath. Collins had apparently prompted him, for he used no more than the

151

name of Scott. They didn't have an official star and Holichek had cut one from the bottom of a tin basin. Then Morse suggested that the first thing Scott should do as the new marshal was get some decent clothes. Mayor Craig gladly extended him the credit, and he went to the General Store and picked out a pair of foxed pants, a pair of kerseymeres, a box-back coat, three broadcloth shirts, and a black string tie. Then he was conducted to his office in front of the temporary jail, a rude log building next door to the T-Rail Saloon.

The blacksmith was busy fitting locks to the three cell doors at the rear and a carpenter was putting a gun rack on the front wall. The trustees took their leave, and Scott changed into his new clothes and went to lunch with Collins. After the meal Collins left to close a deal and Scott lingered over a last cup of coffee.

It was bad for him to be alone. He welcomed the rush and bustle that had filled the morning, welcomed Collins's companionship, Penny's sunny presence. They were the things that kept him from thinking too much, from remembering. But now he was alone. He was thinking of all of them, but somehow he was thinking mostly of Feather. Where was he now? That sensitive, laughing kid, reaching out to life like a plant reaching for the sun. And Jade. Where was Jade? He rose abruptly. He couldn't let it go any further. There was no use in letting it go any further. When he was with Penny, he could forget her. Jade had been wrong for him, and Penny was right. He was getting as bad as Yankee now. Black and white, right and wrong, nothing in between. . . .

"Jeb," he said, "can you put this on the cuff till the end of the week?"

The shirt-sleeved counterman looked at his tin star. "Sure thing, Marshal."

Through the fly-specked window the street was visible. On the opposite side Taw sauntered into view, stopped under the wooden overhang of the harness shop, leaned against one of the supports, and pulled a cigar from his breast pocket. Then, idly, he surveyed the café.

Scott walked outside. Taw saw him and grinned. As Scott crossed the street, Taw bit off the tip of his cigar and spat it out.

"Afternoon Marshal. Elegant suit."

Scott halted in front of him. "That will be five dollars, Taw."

"What?"

"Expectorating on the sidewalk."

Taw looked blankly at the splintery planks. "What the hell! Just the tip of my cigar."

"You saw him spit on the sidewalk, didn't you, Holichek?"

The smith was just passing them on the walk. He stopped, gaping at Scott. Then he grinned. "Yeah, Marshal. I guess I did."

"Several other witnesses," Scott told Taw. "The fine is five dollars. If you want to contest, you can post a bond. Either way we'll have to see the court clerk."

"You're crazy," Taw said. "There isn't any law against spitting on the sidewalks. You'll have to throw the whole town in jail."

"And you first, Taw. Are you coming?"

"Hell, no."

Scott settled forward. His shoulders took on a deeper slope and the strong sunlight shimmered on the sharp edges of his cheek bones. "I could use force, Taw. I wonder if you and Bannack are in a position to raise a big stink."

Taw hesitated. The blood darkened his face till the mottled scars on his cheeks shone white as chalk. With a disgusted sound, he flung the cigar from him, and stepped from beneath the overhang. Scott walked beside him across the street.

They hadn't built a courthouse yet and Fogerty held his court three times a week in the lobby of the Ute Hotel. When it wasn't in session, the court clerk officiated at the T-Rail. He was a tall, dour Scotsman named Innes, sporting a pince-nez, sleeve protectors, and an alpaca vest. He was playing a game of freeze-out with Morse and three others at a rear table.

"Man wants to pay a fine," Scott said.

Holding his cards in one hand, Innes opened the ledger beside him and took up a goose quill. "What's the charge?"

"Expectorating on the sidewalk."

The quill hovered above the ledger. "Is that on the books?"

"It is," Scott said. "Five dollars."

The quill began to scratch. "You're going to have a mighty clean town, Marshal."

Taw gave his name and paid the five dollars. Then he turned to Scott. "I'll get it back, one way or the other."

"Move along. You're blocking traffic."

"That's against the law, too?"

"Five dollars or one day."

Taw's grin came to his face, giving him the look of silent, sardonic laughter. "Marshal," he said, "you're a card."

CHAPTER FOURTEEN

Scott stood outside the T-Rail watching Taw disappear around the corner. It wasn't the end of it, he knew. But he had drawn first blood, and he could stretch it out as long as they wanted.

He got tobacco and papers on credit from the General Store and rolled himself a cigarette. It was good to have his own makings again. It was good to feel washed and shaved and have decent clothes on his back. He thought of Penny, washing her clothes within a two blocks' walk, and of Collins, spry and friendly, just around the corner, and it filled him with warmth and kinship.

He patrolled the town through the late afternoon and saw that even during the short time he had been here the news of the approaching rails had brought a greater sense of crowded hubbub to the town. The

Murphys and the Espenshieds stood in seemingly endless lines before the warehouses and the mercantiles and the stores, their dusty mules snorting and stamping in sweaty harness, their drivers and swampers working like galley slaves to unload the freight. The Land Office was mobbed, and a constant flow of traffic filled the street—dusty riders and handsome paneled landaus and spring buggies and rattling buckboards. Collins had told him that the town already had more than a thousand people and, as soon as the rails hit, he could multiply that by twenty.

It brought the responsibility of his job fully to him for the first time. He had halted before the Royal Flush to roll another smoke when a man stopped in front of him. He was young, slim, swaggering, a haze of desert dust powdering his black shirt and his foxed pants. He had a pinched face, hollow in the cheeks and drawn about the mouth, and jackal eyes.

"I'm Dobie Hoag," he said. "I hear you need deputies."

Scott looked at the gun slung against his hip, a big Dragoon conversion. Nothing gaudy about it, or synthetic, this was the real article.

"You out for the money?" Scott said. "Or the glory?"

"What's the difference?" Hoag said. "In a few days this town will be plain hell, Marshal. You'll need whatever you can get."

Scott looked into those eyes. They had seen too much but were always looking for more. Maybe he

156

wasn't so unstable as Kalispel, but he had a mean streak and was probably so jumpy on the trigger he'd shoot his own foot off someday. Scott knew the kind too well.

"I'll put your name on the list," he said. "The ones I pick will be posted outside the office in a couple of days."

Hoag hesitated. He must have sensed the decision had already been made for the meanness rose like bile into his eyes. For a moment Scott thought the boy would curse him. Instead, Hoag spat at Scott's feet, and turned to push into the crowd.

"Isn't that against the law, Marshal?" a man asked.

Scott turned to see Judge Fogerty. He had just come out of the Royal Flush, and he looked down at the sidewalk with a wry smile. Scott followed the glance to the wet toe of his own boot.

"Looks like it didn't reach the sidewalk," he said. "Next time I'll have to move my foot."

Fogerty sighed. "Why do the murderers always get off on a technicality?"

Scott grinned wryly at the man. All at once a wild whooping arose from the edge of town, making them both look eastward. Scott saw a wagon loaded with men, then a bunch of galloping riders, then another wagon. The men began dropping off the wagon as soon as they entered town, shouting and running for the nearest saloon.

Fogerty moved over beside Scott. "Looks like your job's begun, Marshal."

Scott nodded. The railroad was here. These were the advance guard, the graders who worked twenty or thirty miles ahead of the tracks. Half a block down a man dropped off a wagon and started running for the T-Rail. He was six feet tall, had a frayed cigar in his mouth, and was broad through the shoulders. He was almost at the saloon when he saw Scott. He stopped, blinked, and then let out a braying shout.

"*Arragh!*" he bawled. "It can't be!" He looked like a charging bull. "Begor!" Traffic spread from him in a panic and two pedestrians who didn't jump soon enough got knocked off their feet. "Scott, you Dubh gaill, you black, loquacious, tale-telling Firbolg. . . ."

He was on Scott then, pounding him on the back and whirling him around and shouting like a madman. Behind him came the rest of the crew. Con Dempsey and Paddy Creedon and Bill Figgis and Teigue Flannery and Tom Monahan, pumping his hand and battering him with clouts and bringing others with their shouts.

"Don't tell me you're grading now!" Scott shouted.

"Hell, no!" Mickey Dan yelled. "We couldn't wait. Nothin' since Benton. Nothin' but hot porter and blindin' dust and howlin' redskins. 'I got t'have the burn o' good whiskey,' I says to the Quinn. 'I got t'have the feel of a woman in my hands.' 'Go to it,' he says. 'Let the freighters take ye in. Never let it be said that them graders got t'the wimen and the whiskey before the Quinn's men.' " Mickey Dan caught Scott by both shoulders and held him at arm's length. "And

158

what does the little tin star make you?"

"Marshal," Scott said. "I'm supposed to keep you from wrecking the town."

"Wrecking is it?" Mickey Dan threw back his head and emitted a deafening laugh. "When we get through, there won't be no town left to wreck. Now come in and have the first drink with me. One gallon o' whiskey, one fresh cigar, and then I'm a-going to fight every grader in Green River."

The rush of them took him through the batwings into the saloon. Mickey Dan set them up and for a while Scott forgot his duty, surrounded by the brogue of them and listening to all the new Dan Casement jokes and the incredible bragging. Mickey Dan had emptied most of the bottle when a grader's voice rose above the babble.

"Where the hell would them rail layers be without us? We carve out a track bed for 'em while they're havin' their tea like a ladies' sewin' circle, chew up the Indians for 'em while they're hidin' in their sleepin' cars, whittle down the weather for 'em so it won't give 'em. . . ."

"And do a damn' poor job of all three!" Mickey Dan bellowed.

The grader wheeled around, a bottle in one hand. He was a big man, tawny-maned, with desert dust caked like powder on his broad face. "You should know about poor jobs," he said. "I hear the Central Pacific's laying fifteen miles a day."

Mickey Dan hit the bar so hard it shuddered. Then

he plucked his frayed cigar from his mouth, flipped it at a brass spittoon, and pointed to a box of stogies on the back-bar shelf.

"One o' them long black ones, thank you."

He bent forward so the barman could thrust the cigar between his teeth. Con Dempsey already had a match lit. Scott grasped Mickey Dan's arm.

"Hold it, Mickey. This is exactly what I've got to stop."

Mickey Dan dragged deep, lighting his cigar, and flayed an arm out, pushing Scott free. "Stop it tomorrow night. These graders have been talkin' too big too long."

Scott caught himself, grabbed for the man's arm. "Mickey. . . ."

But the big Irishman lunged away from him, wading through the press for the grader. "You'll retract your allegations," he said. "No rail crew in history ever laid fifteen miles a day."

"You're a liar!" the grader said.

The grader was lifted from his feet by a roundhouse blow that deposited him his full length away from Mickey Dan. He rolled over, shaking his head dazedly, and scrambled back onto his feet.

Scott pulled his gun and jammed hard through the press, knowing he had to stop this quick or it would turn into a regular Donnybrook. He saw a grader jump onto the bar with a chair in his hands, clubbing Con Dempsey down with it. At the same time Mickey Dan rushed that grader he had dazed, swinging another

roundhouse that landed on the side of the man's head. It staggered him and almost drove him to his knees, swinging him around till his back was toward Scott. It blocked off Mickey Dan. As the grader spread his feet, shouting in stunned rage, and started to throw himself back at Mickey Dan, Scott hit him across the back of the neck with his gun barrel. The man grunted and pitched forward like a felled ox.

"Now," bawled Scott, "you'll keep your fights to camp! The next man that starts a brannigan . . . !"

The grader on the bar threw the chair. It struck Scott full in the face, cutting off his shout. He went backward, falling into the mob. They gave way, and he slumped heavily to the floor.

Dazed from the blow, he tried to sit up. His face was bleeding and he had trouble making his muscles work. A knee caught him in the ribs. A man kicked at somebody else and Scott's face was in the way. It was like an explosion in his head, agony, flashing lights, numbness, all at once.

He pawed blindly at their surging legs, arms held in front of his face to protect it. He got to his knees, and then a man fell across him, driving him down again. Part of the crowd was rushing toward the door and they trampled across him like a herd of stampeding horses. Beaten, in a stupor of pain, he crawled toward the bar. There was a crash of the mirror breaking and glass showered down on him. Buffeted back and forth, beaten down whenever he tried to rise, he crawled over an inert body. He saw that it was Bill Figgis. His

161

mouth gaped open and all his front teeth had been kicked out.

He reached the gleaming brass rail, reached up for the bar. Sick and groaning, he hauled himself up. He hung over the bar, wanting to retch, unable to move for a moment. He had a crazy glimpse of a grader knocking Tom Monahan through a front window. Then Paddy Creedon picked the grader up bodily and heaved him after Monahan. A deal table went over with a crash and flames from a lamp began to lick up a side wall.

A bartender came staggering through the débris of smashed furniture and fallen bodies, laying about him wildly with the business end of a loaded cue.

"For God's sake, Marshal, stop 'em!" he shouted. "I was at Benton when they rioted. They'll have this town torn up in ten minutes if you don't stop 'em. . . ."

Scott shook his head. Everything was fuzzy. He couldn't think and he couldn't make his feet move right and he didn't even have a gun.

He turned and almost fell on his face. Stumbling, pushed back and forth by the fighting men still in the room, he tried to gain the door. A thrown bottle barely missed his head and broke against the bar. He was knocked down twice before he reached the door. He saw that it had spread all over the street now, hundreds of graders fighting hundreds of rail layers. Wagons were upturned with their freight spilled in heaps; most of the windows for the length of a block had been smashed; a six-hitch team had broken loose and was

running crazily through the mob, whale-oil lamps had been pulled down, and the saloon was already on fire.

Fogerty came running down the walk, his coat almost torn off him, his face bleeding. He saw Scott and wheeled into him, grabbing his arms.

"How did you let this get started, man? What kind of a marshal are you? Do something. I'll get Morse and Holichek. Those rifles in your office. . . ."

"We can't do that," Scot said. "It'll start a massacre."

"We've got to stop it somehow!" Fogerty yelled. "They're going crazy! If they spread much farther up the street, it'll be the women and children."

"Have you got a fire truck?"

"In Holichek's barn. Just brought it in from the East."

"Find me a dozen men. We'll roll it down here."

Scott stumbled across the walk and shoved his shoulder against a knot of frantically shouting men. He saw Morse run from the Land Office with a shotgun and shouted at him. He swung his arm down the street toward Holichek's livery and Morse came at a run. In front of the café by his office he saw Collins, shouting and struggling on the fringe of another battle. He called to the man, and Collins started running. The mob was thinning out to a few scattered individual battles by the time they reached Holichek's. The smith stood like the Colossus of Rhodes before the yawning door of his barn; he had a twenty-pound sledge across his chest and his biceps were knotted with muscle.

"Some Irishman's going to get a busted head," he announced.

"Roll out the engine!" Scott shouted. "Get it down by that big trough in front of the Tie-Camp!"

Holichek looked at him blankly, then he wheeled to lead them into the dark barn. Scott followed his tramping feet and found the shafts in the darkness. With no time to hitch up a team, the men pulled it out. They were met at the door by Fogerty and half a dozen other townsmen. Only when they passed outside did Scott see the truck. The huge hand-power pump was concealed in an ornate body of gleaming brass and silver scrollwork, mounted on four large, slender-spoked wheels with brass hub caps. They charged into the seething mob of railroaders like a squadron of cavalry, the heavy truck scattering men right and left. There were a score of townsmen around the engine by the time they reached the long trough before the Tie-Camp.

They swung it up beside the trough, and, while Fogerty tapped into the water, Holichek attached the leather hose. The operating power was provided by handrails on each side, long enough for twelve men apiece. Scott took his place with others at the rail and Morse jumped atop the wagon.

"Down with the right!" he bawled.

Twelve men threw their weight onto the bar. The right rail went down and the left rail went up and an embryonic stream of water filtered from the hose.

"Down with the left."

164

The other twelve men pushed on their bar. The left rail went down and the right one went up. With more water sucked up by the pump, the stream from the hose was stronger. It splattered the nearest group of battling railroaders.

"Down . . . down . . . down. . . ."

The pumpers found their rhythm and the tempo picked up. The water began to spray out with force, pressing half a dozen of the battling men backward, then knocking some off their feet. It broke up the fight and left them standing stupidly in the street, soaked to the skin, surprised, gaping foolishly at one another. Holichek turned the spray on the men fighting along the sidewalk. It pinned some of them against the wall, swept others through the door. The sweat poured off Scott. His eyes bulged and he was gasping for breath; he knew he couldn't last much longer. More townsmen were gathering around the engine, and, when he staggered away from the rail, too spent for another pump, a fresh man took his place. Scott sagged against the end of the engine, sobbing for air. He saw that the trough was rapidly being emptied.

"Get some buckets!" Morse shouted. "Form a line to that trough in front of the Land Office. We got to keep it going."

Men spread in every direction for buckets, and in a few minutes they were back. Tin pails, bull-hide buckets, wooden kegs, a line of them extending from the engine to a new trough. It gave the truck more mobility. When the powerful spray had broken up the

165

fights near the Tie-Camp, a dozen men got behind the engine and pushed it up the street, with the pumpers still working and Holichek still aiming his devastating stream. Scott saw that it was breaking up the riot, and, when the truck was opposite Collins's realty office, he ducked inside, finding the man's shotgun racked above his bed. He ran out with it and approached the first bunch of soaked graders down the street.

"Get back to camp now," he said. "You're through here for now." He saw Mickey Dan and shouted at the man. "Get your crew out of here! If this happens again, I'll throw the whole lot of you in jail!"

Mickey Dan was soaked to the skin, shaking water off like a half-drowned spaniel. "What the hell, Scott, me boy! Man's got to let off a little steam now and then."

"Not this way. You've wrecked half the town. Get a move on."

Shivering in the chilly air, they moved eastward along the street. The humor of it had reached most of them now. They were laughing and horseplaying as they walked to their wagons and horses. They were like a bunch of schoolboys after a spree, but the shotgun packed an authority that kept them on the move.

"It's a good idea, Marshal!" Paddy Creedon shouted. "Next time put some whiskey in that engine. We won't even bother with the saloons."

With the first bunch on their way out, Scott turned back. The truck had moved clear up the street now, with the bucket brigade extended out twice as long, a double line of men passing the full pails up and the empty ones back. The street was a muddy mess. Scores of graders and rail layers stood around in the muck or sat blankly on the curbs, their whiskey and their desire for battle soaked out of them by the stunning spray. Every trough and water butt within three blocks had been emptied by the time peace was restored.

When the last rail layers had been headed into the desert, the pumpers staggered to the curb and sat down or threw themselves flat on the splintery walks, utterly spent. Scott caught sight of Penny pushing her way through the crowd of women and townsmen that had gathered at the west end to watch the fight. She saw him and ran through the shambles in the street, pushing her tousled hair off her face in a gesture half of fear, half of relief.

"Scott, Scott, are ye hurt?"

"Just a little battered."

She stopped before him, eyes dark with concern. "Y'r head. It's bleedin'."

It was good to have somebody care. "Nothing really serious, Penny."

She wiped futilely at the blood and the muck on his face, looking off toward the desert. "Those mor mokes," she said. "The Quinn'll dock 'em a week's pay. Swillin' their shebeen and goin' wild like a bunch o' redskins and spoilin' the town f'r decent people."

Scott looked about him, surveying the wreckage.

Aside from taking the fight out of the railroaders, the water had put out the fire that had started at the T-Rail. The whole front wall was blackened and charred and every window in the place had been broken. Almost every other building within three blocks had suffered a like amount of damage, walls smashed in, doors torn off and thrown into the street, the kindling of broken furniture strewn across the walks. Throughout the same area almost every wagon in sight was over-turned, spilling freight onto the ground. Flour bags had split open, sifting their powdery cargo into the mud, and a thousand tin cans littered the street.

Morse came out of his Land Office. "They tore up half the plats in the place. We'll be having title trouble for a hundred years."

Mayor Craig waded through the muck and stopped by Scott. His face was beet-red from pumping and his handsome marseille waistcoat was smeared with mud. He stared at the freight heaped in the street before his General Store, half of it tramped into the mud by the mob.

"A thousand dollars' worth of it, Scott, and I'll be lucky to salvage a hundred."

Bobo Tanner, the operator of the T-Rail, came through the door of his wrecked saloon, wiping blood from his face. He looked at the charred wall and then glared at Scott.

"It'll cost me a fortune to repair the damage here. What the hell did we hire you for? If it's gonna be this way every night, we better get a new marshal."

168

Fogerty was a few feet away. He walked to them, looking at Craig, at Morse. All the wry humor was gone from his age-pleated face.

"Tanner's right, gentlemen," he said. "I think we'd better have a meeting about this in the morning."

CHAPTER FIFTEEN

When Scott awoke next morning, his body ached from the battering it had taken, his head throbbed, and the thought of food nauseated him. He walked with Collins through the shambles still left from the night before. A hot morning sun was sucking moisture from the damp ground and it steamed up like fog about the men still scrounging around in the street for the last of the muddy, trampled freight. A pair of carpenters had erected a scaffold and were tearing out the burned wall of the T-Rail. Mayor Craig's clerk was sweeping broken glass into a heap behind gaping windows. Through the open door of the Land Office, Scott saw Morse on his knees, gathering up a mess of ruined ledgers and papers.

"I don't blame them if they fire me," Scott said.

"Take it easy," Collins said. "It's a new job to you. None of them could have done any better. I think you can handle it if they'll give you a chance."

"I've got some ideas," Scott admitted.

"Then I'll fight for you."

Collins ate breakfast but all Scott could down was three cups of coffee, bitter and black. When they stepped from the café, he saw Ed Cabinet standing across the street.

The meeting had been called for ten that morning in the tack room of Holichek's barn. They were all there, Mayor Craig and Judge Fogerty and Morse and Holichek and the others, sitting around the crude table. And Hi Bannack.

When he saw Scott, he settled back in his chair, blandly confident. His hands were flat on the table, with their fan-like pattern of sinews beneath the freckled flesh, their tufts of rusty hair behind each massive knuckle joint.

Scott stopped beside Mayor Craig, nodding at Bannack. "New trustee?"

Craig had to speak loudly to be heard above the hubbub of argument. "Mister Bannack is here representing the railroad. They want a peaceful town as much as we do."

Gordon Simms, the city contractor, stood at the other end of the table, pounding on its top and arguing heatedly with Morse. "A hundred armed men covering the head of every street could seal the whole town off from those railroaders."

"And your town would die," Bobo Tanner said. "These railroaders are going to supply ninety percent of your income for the next month. In Cheyenne, even the legitimate operators were making twenty and thirty thousand dollars a week. All you need is a marshal that's willing to use his gun."

"You'd start a worse riot than you had last night,"

170

Collins said. "These graders would come back with their own guns."

"This town wouldn't be in existence without those rails," Scott told them. "These railroaders aren't outlaws to be shot down in the streets."

"Give Scott a chance to get organized," Collins pleaded. "He was only one day in the office. He didn't even have any deputies."

Bannack exhaled smoke into the blue haze filling the room. "An experienced man would have had his organization. I suggest you get a new marshal, gentlemen. Might I nominate Ed Cabinet?"

"I second," Bobo Tanner said.

A roar of protest went up from Craig and the other businessmen in the room.

"That gunman?" Simms said. "We might as well turn the town over to the railroaders."

Bannack grinned blandly. "Can you suggest somebody else?"

There was an uncomfortable muttering among the group. Finally Collins smiled humorlessly. "You have just been presented with the facts of life, gentlemen."

"We'll find a man," Simms muttered, "even if we have to import one of those town-tamers from farther east."

"And in the meantime what are you going to do for law in Green River?" Collins asked.

Again they were stumped. They muttered and argued among themselves till Craig finally slapped the table. "The chair moves that we retain Marshal Scott

171

until other arrangements have been made."

"Second the motion," Morse said.

Bannack ground his cigar out against the table, staring through the blue-gray smoke at Scott. His blue eyes were slitted, baleful, calculating. Scott knew what he was weighing. He could almost feel the clash, as their glances met.

You talk, Bannack, and so will I. Scott might as well have said it. He could see the understanding in Bannack's face, and the angry resignation. The others rose and drifted to the door, embarrassed, avoiding Scott's eyes. Bannack put both broad hands against the table, pushed his chair back, and rose. As he passed, Scott murmured: "Too bad, Bannack."

None of the others was close enough to hear. Bannack paused, smiling malevolently. "I'll give you the rope, Scott. You'll hang yourself soon enough. One more night with those railroaders and you'll be through."

He walked on, and Collins joined Scott. "A helluva shabby way to treat a man that's willing to risk his life for them," he said. "If I were you, I'd turn in my star and let 'em stew in their own juice."

"Can't blame 'em," Scott said. "Maybe I can make 'em change their minds before they find a new man."

Collins's eyes settled on Bannack's broad back, just walking through the door. "And what about him?"

"Stalemate, so far."

"It can't go on. Something's got to give."

"Have you found out anything new?" Scott asked.

"Nothing. I was up on the Palisades yesterday again.

172

Went over every square foot. Not a thing."

"Written to Omaha?"

"And Washington. If those plats have been juggled, we'll find out." He shook his head angrily. "Why can't we just blow off the lid? Why can't we tell Craig and the trustees what Bannack's doing to their town?"

"What is he doing?"

Collins snorted. "I know, I know. I was just blowing off a little steam."

"We've got to hang on, Collins. If we get Bannack nervous enough, it might give us a lead."

They passed through the dusky barn, with its smells of manure and hay and sweating horseflesh. The forge fire was a core of yellow light in the gloom, shimmering across the ripple and bulge of Holichek's bare biceps as he shaped a red-hot shoe. Over the clang of his hammer he called to Scott.

"The whole board ain't ag'in' you, Marshal! You want a part-time deputy, jist call on me when them railroaders hit town."

Scott grinned at him. "Thanks, Holichek."

Outside, the eastward windows of a dozen buildings blazed yellow in the sunlight. Morning shadows lay cold and blue in the notches between the frame structures and across the street, sitting on the tie rail of the café, was Ed Cabinet.

"The morning shift," Scott said bitterly.

Collins stopped. "Are they still watching you?"

"Either that or trying to break my nerve," Scott said. "And I don't like either."

173

Collins touched his arm. "Don't push your luck."

"I'm still marshal," Scott said. "Sooner or later they're going to believe that."

He left Collins and walked directly across the street to Cabinet. The man rose from the rack.

"Rough night, Marshal."

Scott stopped in front of him, so close their faces were less than a foot apart. "I don't like to be watched, Cabinet."

"I'm just standing here."

"In other words, you won't move on?"

"Why should I? There ain't no law against what I'm doing."

"Yes, there is."

"What law?"

"Lying in the street gets you fifteen dollars or five days."

"I'm just standing here. . . ."

"You're lying in the street. Judge Fogerty's holding court in the Ute Hotel. You can come and pay your fine there."

"I ain't lying in the street, damn you!"

"Yes, you are. I've got a dozen witnesses. Now are you coming easy or hard?"

"I ain't coming and I ain't paying no fine. I'm just standing here like any peaceful, law-abidin' citizen. . . ."

Scott put the heel of his gun against the man's chest and pushed. It jammed Cabinet's hips against the tie rack and flipped him over like a tenpin. He fell on his back in the dust between rack and curb. With a curse he tried to roll over, grabbing for his own gun. Scott scissored the rack and dropped onto the other side, jamming one boot down on Cabinet's wrist. It pinned the man there, his face twisted with pain. Scott stooped and tore the gun from his helpless hand. Then, straddling Cabinet, with his boot still pinning one wrist to the ground, Scott asked Collins: "Did you see this man lying in the street?"

Collins had crossed behind Scott and stood five feet out from the rack. A mischievous grin sent a spider web of creases into his cheeks.

"Couldn't call it anything else, could you?"

Scott looked at Cabinet. "You going to pay that fine?"

Cabinet was still writhing on the ground, trying to get his wrist from beneath Scott's boot. "I won't pay no fine, damn you!"

Scott grinned balefully. "Then I guess you'll go to jail."

It helped Scott's humor to have a prisoner in the jail. It seemed to make everything official. He felt more like a marshal now and went about his duties with a greater sense of authority. Before lunch he got a man to paint him ten big signs. Five of them said GRADERS and five of them said RAIL LAYERS. After lunch he went around and hung them up on the façades of the ten saloons in town. The T-Rail was last. The carpenters had torn down the charred wall and were building a new one. Scott hung his sign at the other end of the

175

wooden awning, where it could be seen by anyone approaching from the east. While he was at work, Bobo Tanner came out and stood scowling at Scott.

"What's that for?"

"Get a grader and a rail layer together and you're always going to end up with a fight," Scott said. "So we're going to separate 'em. From now on you're catering solely to graders."

"You'll cut my business in half."

"You'll make just as much money. I'm trying to keep your place from being wrecked again, Tanner. Are you going to fight me on this, too?"

Tanner rubbed at his greasy jowls viciously. "If this doesn't work out, Marshal, I'll take your job myself."

Scott gave him a bleak grin and started back to his office. There was a man waiting for him, filling Scott's chair with his massive frame, puffing impatiently on his cigar. Hi Bannack.

Scott stopped just inside the doorway and Bannack leaned back in the swivel chair, bringing a creak from the rusty springs. He tilted the cigar upward in his mouth and surveyed Scott from head to foot, then made a disgusted sound.

"Box-back coat, English pants, fancy shirt. You look fine. Just fine."

Their whole relationship had become so ironic that Scott wanted to laugh. But then he thought of the dark things behind them, the twisted things, the killing and the lives ruined—and the humor was quenched in him.

"A thorn in your side, Bannack?"

Without answering, Bannack ground his cigar out against the top of the desk. He seemed to take a perverted delight in making as big a burn scar as possible. "Somebody tells me you've got Ed Cabinet in the tank now," he said.

"He wouldn't pay his fine," Scott answered. "It finally came out he didn't have any money on him. I guess he was ashamed to send a message to you."

"Why? What's the charge?"

"Lying in the street."

Bannack let his breath out with an explosive sound. "What kind of charge is that?"

"It's on the books. Fifteen dollars or five days."

Bannack was silent for a moment, studying Scott's face, gauging him. Finally: "What are you doing, Scott?"

Scott's voice lowered, became sibilant. "As long as you keep putting your dogs on me, Bannack, I can keep tying cans to their tails."

Anger turned Bannack's face a shade paler and the freckles looked almost black against his cheeks. His breathing took on a wheezing sound and he spoke in a thick voice. "You're not that safe."

"As safe as you are, Bannack."

The man came up out of the chair, his glittering eyes trying to pierce Scott's possessed calm. "If you know so much, why don't you talk, why don't you spill it?"

"Why do you think, Bannack?"

The man settled back. The anger seeped out of him,

and he tucked his thumbs under his lapels, a malicious gleam coming to his eyes. He didn't have to say anything. Scott could almost read his mind. The picture was obvious to both of them. Scott couldn't expose Bannack without putting himself in the hands of the law and he'd be indicted for complicity in Riordan's murder.

"All right." Bannack circled the desk, hanging on to his lapels, scowling at the floor. "What's it getting you? You're just sitting on the edge of the razor. You can't hope for anything permanent here, with that always hanging over your head."

"Can you?"

Bannack glanced at him sharply, stopped his pacing. He frowned at the window, as if coming to a decision. Then: "If I made a statement absolving you of all possible complicity in Riordan's murder, would you clear out of here?"

"No."

Bannack looked at him again, anger quickening in his face. He snorted. "I can't clear your father. After all, he did kill Riordan."

"I know that."

"What do you want, Scott? What in hell do you want?"

Scott measured the man. "I don't know yet, Bannack. I don't exactly know."

Little muscles bunched up around Bannack's compressed lips and his eyes were squinted with frustrated anger. He was about to speak again when boots clattered on the walk and a shadow fell across the

178

threshold. A tall man followed it, a tall man in a Texas-creased Stetson and a black alpaca coat and pants powdered white with desert dust. He had gray eyes, creviced by perpetual watchfulness at the corners, and a gray face, drawn about the mouth and set in a hard shape. He took off his hat and slapped it once against his leg. His hair was yellow as new hemp and clipped short about the ears. He looked at Bannack.

"Marshal Scott?"

Bannack nodded at Scott. "There."

The man turned to Scott, slipping a wallet from inside his coat and opening it to reveal his identification. "Marshal John Olvis, United States government," he said.

It struck Scott with definite impact. He heard Bannack's boots make a sharp little scrape against the pine floor. There was a pause that seemed to stretch out forever, and then Scott recovered and mechanically held out his hand. He heard his voice, as if from a great distance: "Glad to meet you, Olvis."

Olvis's hand held a sinewy strength. He put the wallet back and Scott had a glimpse of an underarm harness and the glint of a gun butt.

"I'm on the trail of the Walker gang," Marshal Olvis said. "They were last seen in Benton, heading west. Do you have any information?"

It was like a pressure against Scott's chest. It was like gasping for air and not getting enough, and trying all the time to cover up and waiting for Bannack to say something.

"No," Scott said. His voice sounded strained, metallic. "No sign of them here."

The silence came again. Scott knew it lasted only a second, but it seemed a year, a lifetime. His glance swung to Bannack despite himself and he saw the brightness in the man's eyes, the avidness, like a cat ready to pounce on a mouse. This was the moment. If Bannack meant to speak, he would do so now.

It was the same meeting of eyes, the same clash of wills that had come when Scott had seen Bannack at the meeting of the trustees—and that same tacit understanding quivering like a live thing between them. *If you talk, I talk.* Bannack knew. He knew.

Bannack took out his own wallet. "You and the marshal want to talk, Scott. If you'll tell me how much the fine is, I'll leave."

"You'll have to pay the court clerk," Scott said. "Judge Fogerty can send the release over."

Bannack nodded. Then he turned to Olvis, all affability and charm. "I'm Hi Bannack, Marshal. In the surveyor general's office here. If I can be of any assistance, don't hesitate."

Olvis shook hands, completely unimpressed. Bannack went out. Scott glanced at Olvis, then moved to the door. Bannack was about to cross the street.

"Not in the middle of the block, Bannack. That would cost you ten dollars."

Bannack jerked back. Then he scowled at Scott. "How much does it cost to breathe?"

Scott smiled. "If Taw and Cabinet don't mind their

own business, I might get around to that."

"Marshal," Bannack said, "when you're gone from that office, I just won't know what to do for a hobby."

He tramped off toward the corner, the plank walk clattering and popping beneath his solid weight. Scott looked at Olvis and waved at the chair. The government marshal put his hat on the desk and folded his lean length into the chair. Scott placed his back to the wall, trying to hide the tension in him, saying: "How does the government get in on this? The *Index* played up the Walker affair as strictly local."

Olvis looked at him quizzically. "The man the Walkers killed was a United States marshal."

"Riordan? I thought he was a tie contractor."

"That was just a front," Olvis said. "Most of his work was under cover. You know how close the government and the railroad are working to get these rails down, Scott. In such a big operation there's going to be a lot of chance for graft. Riordan was originally commissioned to break up a land swindle in Omaha. Then he was kept on to help prevent the same thing recurring. His last report indicated he'd come across something big in Laramie. What it was he never got to tell us."

"Do you think it was connected with the Walkers?"

Olvis took out a jackknife, opened it, and began cleaning his nails. "I don't know. The Walkers hadn't perfected title to that land. Time I got there another homesteader had filed on it."

"What was his name?"

"Kalispel."

Scott turned his back and walked to the window, not trusting his face any longer, not trusting his control on his reactions. He took out his makings and rolled a smoke and tried to keep his fingers from trembling. He could add most of it up, could see how Bannack had retained control of Cheyenne Parks and still had covered himself there so that even Olvis couldn't unearth any evidence. But if the relationship between Bannack and Kalispel could be established. . . .

Scott lit his cigarette, filled for a moment with the impulse to tell Olvis everything, to take a chance. What he could add to the man's knowledge might be what they needed to break the thing wide open. Then the doubts began pressuring him. He could not prove Kalispel worked for Bannack, even though he knew it himself. He didn't even have any positive proof of what Bannack was doing here. No papers had been signed yet. Taw had surely covered himself as carefully here as Bannack had in Laramie. On the surface everything was legitimate. It would simply be Collins's word against theirs, and no evidence of any sort.

The thought occurred to him that he should tell Olvis his suspicions about the Palisades deal without revealing his own identity. He rejected it immediately. Olvis might go to Bannack and that would tip Bannack off that Scott had talked, and Bannack might expose Scott in reprisal.

The stalemate worked both ways. But if he was in a corner, so was Bannack. He had the man on the defen-

182

sive now. If he put himself in Marshal Olvis's hands, he would be helpless. He had to hang on. His only hope was that something would break soon enough to give him a lead, a chance.

The whole process had gone through his mind in but a few moments. Dragging on his cigarette, he turned to glance at Olvis. Those gray eyes, those cold gray eyes, were probing into him.

"It's funny," Olvis said. "One of the boys in the gang is named Scott Walker."

Cotton was in Scott's mouth. The blood was so thick in his throat he could hardly speak. His lips were stiff as cement as he tried to convey a rueful smile. "Don't rub it in, Marshal."

The man didn't answer the smile. "You Scotch?"

"Irish."

"Don't look Irish."

"Sir Walter Scott was an Irishman."

Marshal Olvis closed his jackknife and tucked it away. "I'll be staying at the Ute Hotel. You hear anything, let me know."

He walked out and headed down toward the corner. Scott saw that Bannack was still down there, thumbs under his lapels, talking with Morse. Olvis stopped beside them and Bannack spoke to him, a long sentence, frowning and pulling at his lapels. When he was finished, Olvis looked back toward Scott. Then he said something to Bannack, and they both disappeared around the corner.

CHAPTER SIXTEEN

It was known that Scott wanted deputies and in the afternoon he began to get applicants. Before six o'clock a dozen men had come to his office and he had chosen five. The best of the lot was Charlie Duncan, an ex-shotgun guard for Wells Fargo. He had lost an arm in a coach accident but he could still handle a sidearm and had a formidable reputation among the stagecoachers. There were a pair of drifters—Sam Watkins and Hay Karns—cowmen who had lost a road herd to Indians on the way to Cheyenne and who needed a job badly. They were dirty and tattered and looked like a pair of tramps but Scott had learned to judge men in the Army. They had hard, strong faces and steady eyes and they had come through a lot of hell with the herd and it had neither broken their nerve nor made them loud and boastful. He thought they were the kind who would be good in a fight and he signed them on.

The fourth man called himself G.G. Nickerson. He was five feet tall and almost as broad, and Scott had seen him whip two graders twice his size in the saloon brawl the night before. The fifth was Holichek, willing to work a half shift, from six o'clock on.

It seemed like a farce, a stupid little mockery for Scott to go about these duties, when any minute the whole thing might blow up in his face. He was like a man walking a fence, waiting to be pushed off with every step. Yet, if he meant to stay, he had to go through the motions.

So at five o'clock, with the shadows long in the streets, he had the deputies haul the fire engine down to the saloon section, parking it in the notch between the Ute Hotel and the Tie-Camp Bar, pulling a buckboard in front to hide it. Then he gave each of the men two saloons to patrol and told them their main duty was to keep the graders and rail layers where they belonged. He had time for dinner and was walking back to the café when a rider trotted past and pulled into the rack before the Royal Flush. It was Taw, his broad, battered face chalky with dust. He dismounted and made his tie and stood by the horse, peering at Scott.

Scott crossed to him and stopped a foot from the man, lifting the sweaty saddle blanket. Taw was a heavy rider. There were gall sores around the cinch and under the tree.

"You beefsteak a horse something awful," Scott said. "Cruelty to animals is ten dollars or five days, Taw."

The man pushed back his hat, took out a handkerchief, and wiped sweat from his brow. "Don't push it too hard, Marshal. Bannack's called off his dogs."

"I'm glad to hear that," Scott said. "Just keep moving when you see me on the street. I'd hate to think you were watching me again."

He crossed the street, and turned north at the intersection, toward the café now, the office, Holichek's

185

livery. Crossing the mouth of the alley opposite the T-Rail, he realized it was the same alley he'd been in when Taw and Cabinet had bracketed him for that first meeting with Bannack. Out of the alley came a voice.

"Scott."

He stopped, with the shock of it seeming to run through his whole body. A woman's voice, soft, throaty, holding a sensual huskiness he could never forget. He wheeled and walked into the alley, seeing her first as a smoky shape in the distant darkness. Each step toward her brought greater definition to her body. The impudent breasts, swelling tautly against a man's shirt, the line of her hips and the curve of her thighs giving columnar roundness to a pair of greasy man's jeans. The face in the darkness was a thing of haunting shadows and satiny crevices, eyes big and dark and startled. He stopped before her, unable to believe it. Then the impulse ran through him to take her in his arms, and yet something held him a foot away from her, rigid, staring, helpless.

It was Jade who broke first. She made a little moaning sound of his name and came into his arms. Her face was pressed against his chest and her arms locked her to him and she was trembling and crying.

"Just hold me, Scott, just hold me so tight, it's been so long, just hold me. . . ."

He embraced her tightly with his face buried against her hair. It was dirty and matted but it still had the texture of silk and it brought back a hundred longings, a thousand bittersweet memories. Then the memories

186

focused into one memory, the choice she had made at Rawlins Springs, and all his longings and all his response to her seemed synthetic and unreal and pointless.

The trembling of her body stopped at last. She became stiff and unyielding in his arms. She pulled free and took a step away, putting her back close to the clapboard wall of the building. The moment of union had gone.

"I'm sorry." Her chin was high and she was biting her lip. "I guess it was just the shock of seeing you."

"You didn't know I was here?" Talking. Stupid, prosaic talking. Covering what they wanted to say with other words. Yet what did they *really* want to say?

"No," she said, answering his question, pushing her hair off her tear-stained face and struggling for control. "I didn't dream you were here. I came after a doctor."

Everything else was driven from him by a sudden fear. "Not the kid . . . ?"

"No," she said. "Feather's all right. It's Noah's old wound. He was hit in the arm when Harvey . . . when Harvey Kane caught up with us that night after Laramie. We finally got Noah to a doctor after Rawlins Springs. Either the man didn't probe all of it out or there were two bullets. Noah's had trouble ever since. His arm's all puffed up again and he's been delirious all day."

"Where are you?"

"In a cabin about ten miles up the Green."

187

"I'll get the doctor. I'll go with you. . . ."

He broke off. He had spoken on impulse. Now he glanced over his shoulder, toward the street.

"What is it?" she asked.

"I'd forgotten," he told her. "I've got a job to do here. I'm city marshal."

"You?" She sounded incredulous.

"I guess it sounds crazy. By all rights I should be running, like you. I did for a long time. But I've got a chance here, Jade. It might be for all of us."

She stood rigidly against the wall, moving her head from side to side like someone in pain. "But surely you can come tonight, Scott. Just a few hours. I'm not asking for myself. It's for them. It isn't just Noah. It's everything. I can't do it myself. You don't know how it's been these last months. Like animals, hounded, running, never getting enough to eat, never getting enough sleep, blamed for a hundred crimes we never committed. Yankee's worse. I thought he'd straighten out, once we got away from Laramie. But he's got something in his mind about Bannack. Something twisted, Scott. I'm at the end of my rope. I can't handle it any longer. I ran into Harvey Kane on my way here. He's at a surveyor cabin. I stopped there because I saw a light. I didn't want to tell him anything, but I did. He's changed, Scott. He hasn't openly broken with Bannack, but he knows now that something dishonest is behind what happened in Laramie. He told me how to get here and that there is a doctor. It was hard for me to leave. I was no longer sure whether I was going to come down here to get the doctor or just keep on going. . . ."

It was like something spilling out of her, all the pain and bitterness and fear of these last months. He saw the strain in her, saw how close she was to breaking. He was torn now between duty and devotion, and yet which was duty, and which devotion? He had his ties here, too, his obligations. Penny, Collins, Holichek, all those who had believed in him, who had stood beside him. Yet this was the time when the faith his family had in him stood or fell. He couldn't betray such a trust. He couldn't run out on them.

"Look," he said. "Can't you hold out just tonight? If I send a doctor and some food? I'll come tomorrow as soon as I can."

She studied his face. It was almost totally dark in the narrow alley now and he could barely see her. She nodded slowly, all vitality, all emotion drained from her voice.

"All right," she said.

"About Kane? Do you think he could help? Do you think he might have evidence that would break Bannack's claims against my family?"

"He may have. I'm not sure. I know he asked me to come back to stay with him after I brought the doctor." Her voice was filled with torment. "But it wouldn't be right. There's my duty to Noah. He's still my husband. It wouldn't be right to run out on him . . . on Feather . . . even on Yankee."

"For Christ's sake, what's wrong with you, Jade?"

Scott was suddenly angry. "You say Harvey Kane's the man who shot Noah . . . and now you . . . you'd go and stay with him?"

Jade reacted fiercely. "When I went to live with your family . . . when I came west with them . . . when I thought you were dead and so married Noah . . . do you think I wanted to live the life of an outlaw . . . be hunted like an outlaw? No one's looked out for me since this whole thing started . . . not even you!"

"You didn't wait at Rawlins Springs."

"I wasn't the one who made that decision . . . not alone I didn't. At the time I felt I was doing it for Noah. He was wounded. And I did it for you. I felt that you might be better off on your own. And I was right, wasn't I? Now you're a town marshal and the rest of the Walkers are being hunted like criminals! Where does that leave me? I didn't shoot anybody. Neither did Noah. But we've all been burned with the same brand."

"There's no reward posted for you," Scott shot back, and then wanted to retract it. Jade had made a number of bad decisions. Now, it seemed, she was tempted to make another one. "Come along. I'll fix you up with some supplies."

Mutely she followed him out of the alley and toward Craig's General Store. While she went for her horse, hitched at the edge of town, Scott put in an order for flour, sugar, coffee, bacon, dried apples, and a small bottle of laudanum for Noah.

"Settin' up housekeeping, Marshal?" the clerk asked.

Scott forced an easy grin. "Getting tired of that highway robbery at the café, Al. Think I'll put a four-burner stove in my office and go into business myself."

The clerk chuckled, adding up the bill, and Scott charged it. He carried the supplies outside and helped Jade load them onto her horse. While she held her animal in a dark section of the street, he went to Doc Gandy's house, a cottage at the west end of town near Mrs. Cassidy's. The balding, crotchety sawbones was eating dinner and Scott had to wait. He had told Jade to give him the name of Fannin and to warn the others not to give themselves away, but he knew he would have to go further than that. Gandy was a shrewd man, and, if it was not handled just right, it could get out of control. So Scott decided to get the jump on the doctor's inevitable suspicions.

"She says they're a bunch of settlers by the name of Fannin that got hit by the Arapahoes up on the Green," Scott told him. "But it sounds funny to me. If you see anything suspicious, let me know."

"Damn that Hippocrates," Gandy said. "If I had my way, a doctor wouldn't take a bullet out unless a man could prove he'd never been in jail, came from Pike County, and voted the straight Republican ticket."

Gandy led his horse beside Scott back to where Jade was waiting at the edge of town. She seemed a small, pathetic-looking figure to Scott, up on her big horse, a memory of a lost life, but again he found himself irritated by what he felt was her waywardness. He also wanted to go along, but he fought it. He couldn't do anything for Noah that the doctor couldn't do a whole lot better. It had best wait till tomorrow.

When the doctor mounted, Jade wheeled her horse without speaking and led the way northward out of town. Scott stood in the black street until he could no longer hear the hoof beats. Then he turned and tramped back toward the center of town.

All the uncertainty was gone from him now. More than ever he seemed to partake of Penny's sure judgment of things, had a glimpse of the road ahead, a goal, a job to do and a reason to do it. Part of that job—justifying, if not exonerating, Yankee might be accomplished now through the help of Harvey Kane. But there was no sense overlooking the biggest problem with all this. It wasn't Bannack. Had Yankee killed Bannack, evidence Kane might supply could throw a new light on what had happened. But Yankee had shot a U.S. marshal, working under cover. How would any evidence against Bannack help Yankee out of that murder charge? Quite simply Yankee in his rage had shot the wrong man and there would still be a terrible price to pay, no matter how legitimate his complaint against Bannack had been.

Before he could go any further in thinking about it, he saw a shadowy figure on the street ahead, stopping at the jail. His name was called, and he answered. The man walked hurriedly toward him. Silhouetted against the diffused illumination of distant lights he made out Garrett Collins's tubby bandy-legged figure.

192

"What is it?" he asked.

"Railroaders are beginning to come in," Collins said. "Charlie Duncan thinks you better see to the T-Rail."

Almost a full block ahead of them Scott could see the agitated forms of a crowd passing across the yellow squares of lighted windows and doorways, could hear the muffled surf of their voices. He moved into a long stride and Collins had to jog to keep up. With only half his mind on the railroaders, he asked: "Bannack bothered you?"

"I had an interview today," Collins said wryly. "Taw and Bannack and that ugly one, Kalispel. They put the pressure on, tried again to get my signature on that lease."

Scott asked sharply: "No rough stuff?"

Collins chuckled. "Not at all. They threatened, but I wouldn't budge. You've got 'em scared, Scott."

"They're not scared of me. Just what they think I know. This United States marshal in town is just that much more pressure. Somebody's got to break, and, if we can stick it out long enough, all that leaves is Bannack."

"But we're so blind. If Bannack does break, what could we look for, how will it come?"

"I've been lying awake nights on that one," Scott said. "I think I have a strong possible lead. I also have had a thought. When a survey is taken, what goes on paper?"

"The field men take their notes in rough draft, right

on the line. Every night the deputy surveyor expands and transfers the notes into his book. The book is delivered to the surveyor general at the end of a job."

"Then, if somebody is juggling this survey, the discrepancy would likely appear between those field notes and the final book."

"It's possible."

"Is Harvey Kane Bannack's field man?" Scott asked.

"Yes. He originally ran the lines on the Palisades and, from what I hear, is now up on the Green."

"What about his notes?"

"Probably with him, but I wouldn't know where to locate him."

"I think I do," Scott said. There was no time for more. They were at the main street and the lights on the wooden overhang of the Tie-Camp Bar spilled saffron channels of light over the tangle of wagons and horses brought in by the first railroad gangs. Dozens of the men were beginning to bank up around the doors of the Tie-Camp and the Royal Flush and the other saloons, shouting and catcalling about the signs Scott had nailed on the overhangs, and more were coming in from the desert.

He saw that the biggest crowd was gathered in front of the T-Rail. Window light splashed dimly against faces he recognized—Billy Figgis, toothless and red-faced, Paddy Creedon, Con Dempsey. Someone was shouting in the front ranks of the crowd. Scott recognized Mickey Dan's stentorian tones.

"And who the divil has the right t'tell us what saloon we can use? If anybody's gonna be kept from their whiskey, it should be thim pulin' graders."

As Scott skirted the crowd and gained the sidewalk in front of the saloon, Charlie Duncan's voice answered, stolid and phlegmatic. "Nobody's bein' kept from their whiskey. You got your saloons, the graders got theirs."

Scott saw the one-armed ex-stagecoacher standing before the batwings, feet spread, his hand on the butt of a Colt stuck through his belt. Beside him was Bobo Tanner, wiping sweat from his flabby face.

"Marshal," he said, "you got to take that sign down. If we try to push 'em around like this, they'll just wreck the place again."

Mickey Dan pushed his way confidently onto the sidewalk, thumbs in his belt, displaying a swollen-shut eye like a proud badge of the fight last night. "There ye are, me boy," he said to Scott. "Tell these hooligans to let us in now. T'would be the shame of our lives to have a grader go into a saloon where we couldn't."

"I put up the sign," Scott said.

Mickey Dan's blue-steel jaw dropped. The shouting and the roaring of all the Quinn's crew had died down and they gaped unbelievingly at Scott. Mickey Dan spat.

"A man that worked among us? A man that sang with us and dropped rails with us and drove spikes with us?"

"I'm still with you," Scott said. "I don't want to see you killed. If you start another riot, these townsmen will come down on you with their guns."

"We can bring ours, too."

"That's what I mean. Do you want a blood bath?"

A bland, placating smile spread like oil across Mickey Dan's face. "Now, Scott, me piaste, me fine, upstanding Galway lanabh, ye know we won't git into any more trouble. The Quinn's comin' in to watch over us like a father."

"Two drinks and he'll be in the Donnybrook with you. You can go to the Tie-Camp. That's one of five set apart for you rail layers."

"And drink that damn' shebeen a Dublin gombeen wouldn't touch?" Mickey Dan asked. He pulled up his pants. "Bobo Tanner's the only man that handles a whiskey fit for a rail layer. *Uisgebeatha*. The real thing. None o' that smoke-cured Scotch the Royal Flush tries t'palm off on us. And we're going to have it."

Scott had told Collins he had some ideas about controlling the railroad crews. The fire engine had been one. Keeping the rail layers and graders apart had been another. This was a third.

He knew that in each gang was a leader, and that man was usually the troublemaker in town, the core of an outbreak like last night. If he could reach that core somehow, cripple it, he would be a long way toward his goal, and Mickey Dan was one of those cores.

"You're not going in," Scott said.

Mickey Dan laughed at him. "You can't stop all of us."

"I can stop you."

The shouting of the men stopped again. Mickey Dan's impudent face went blank with surprise. Then he opened his mouth and let the frayed stub of his cold cigar drop from it. Without taking his eyes off Scott, he held out one hand. Con Dempsey stepped up and put a fresh cigar into it. Mickey Dan placed it between his teeth, and Con Dempsey lit it.

"Beggin' y'r pardon," Mickey Dan said. "I'm going in."

"Excuse me," Scott said. "You're not."

With a happy roar Mickey Dan rushed him. Scott saw it coming, the devastating haymaker that had lifted Con Dempsey off his feet, that had deposited the grader full length on the floor last night. In the last moment he ducked under it. He heard the *whoosh* of its passage over his head, and he drove straight and hard for the belly before him.

He thought his fist went clear through Mickey Dan. The Irishman's air left him in an explosion of sound, and he doubled over. His charging body drove Scott back against the wall. Scott was pinned there a moment by the man's dead weight. Then he pulled himself from between Mickey Dan and the wall, wheeling away. Instead of following, Mickey Dan sagged against the wall, still doubled over and hugging his belly, and then slowly slid to the plank walk. His face was slack and putty-colored with shock and he made awesome, retching sounds, trying to breathe. Unbelievably the cigar was still in his mouth.

For a wild moment Scott thought he had finished it again, then and there, as he had before. The crowd was completely silent behind him. Finally, however, the blood began to seep back into the Irishman's face. He rolled over, groaning, and somehow got to his hands and knees. He crouched there sickly, shaking his head, finally looking up at Scott. His eyes were bleary and tinged with blood, the little muscles gone slack about his wet lips. With a broken sound he launched himself at Scott.

He came up off hands and knees in a low, tackling dive. Scott danced backward, trying to dodge his flailing arms, but there was no belly to hit now, and one of the pawing hands caught his leg. He felt himself going backward. Knowing he was gone, he didn't try to fight it. He threw himself off the curb and into the street and rolled to keep away from the man. He came to hands and knees and saw Mickey Dan staggering blindly after him. He drove up and dodged one flailing roundhouse and twisted a shoulder into his blow. His fist went deeply into the belly of the man again. At the same time Mickey's other hand swung an uppercut.

The world exploded. Scott was in mid-air, in a vacuum, with comets and rockets shooting off in his head. Then a jarring blow struck his shoulder blades and the earth shuddered beneath him. He heard the pound of feet and Mickey Dan's roar of rage. He rolled over and blindly tried to gain his feet. He sensed more than saw another one of those roundhouse blows.

He bent almost double, and it went over his head. Then he wheeled away to dodge the uppercut he knew would follow, still too dazed, too blind to risk closing with the man. His vision returning, he backed away from the Irishman, feinting him into his haymakers, dodging, wheeling, waiting for strength to come back, looking for an opening. The crowd gave way before his retreat. Graders had joined it from other saloons and the street was jammed with men, their excited shouting making a diffuse ocean of sound about him.

Mickey missed a blow and spun halfway around, leaving his face wide open. Scott ignored it. He didn't want to break his hand on that primitive head.

Bellowing, the Irishman wheeled back. Scott dropped his guard, and Mickey Dan swung at his face. Scott ducked in under, blocked the following blow, and hooked again into that belly. Mickey Dan jackknifed and tried to grapple. Scott could have struck again, but he danced back.

That was the way of it. Five minutes, ten minutes, fifteen minutes. Scott lost all measure of time. Backing and wheeling and maneuvering around in that street, scuffling up dust till it hung like smoke over the bellowing crowd, working on that belly, always working on it. Twice more a haymaker got through and nearly finished him. One tore his shirt off first and then numbed the whole side of his face. The other hit his chin, almost knocking his head off, and everything went black. How he stayed on his feet, unconscious, he would never know. It must have been reflexes. He came out of it a couple of seconds later, still backing away from the Irishman on legs that felt like matchsticks.

He saw Mickey Dan plunging in to finish him, wheeled aside, and hooked into the exposed belly. The Irishman grunted sickly, covered, and spun away, barely holding himself on his feet. Scott followed, crouched, feinting, dodging, finding an opening, striking. His arms were like lead now and it was agony to breathe. But he could see it was just a matter of time.

Actually Mickey Dan's demise had been written with that first blow. He had never really recovered from it. If Scott hadn't kept hammering at his belly, he might have come back, but the straight jabbing was something new to the Irishman. He couldn't block it and each new blow added a little more shock, a little more destruction. The life was gone from his stomach muscles. It was like hitting a wet bag.

In a last, wounded desperation, Mickey Dan rushed blindly at Scott. Scott ducked one blow, rolled a second off his shoulder, struck for the belly. This time Mickey Dan jackknifed helplessly. He hung there a moment. His lips went slack and the cigar dropped from them. Slowly, majestically, he toppled to the ground.

Scott took a step away. His shirt was torn from his

back and hanging by his belt. His chest was striped and bloody from nail scratches and blows, and there was no feeling to the left side of his face. He planted his feet wide apart so he wouldn't fall from sheer exhaustion and, swaying back and forth, waited for Mickey Dan to rise. But the man lay doubled up on the ground, feebly trying to retch and unable to suck in enough air to do it, a sick Irishman, a very sick, very beaten Irishman.

Scott hated himself for it. Why couldn't there be another way? Why did you have to do that to a man you loved like a brother? He knew Mickey Dan would forgive him in an hour and the hurt would be gone in a day or so. But right now he hated himself.

He surveyed the crowd, a stream of blood leaking from one corner of his mouth. In a gusty voice he asked: "Does any other rail layer want to go into that saloon?"

A soft muttering ran through them, but none answered. They were all staring at Mickey Dan. Their god was down, their mighty fallen. There was more of a defeat in this than they had met last time, even more perhaps than in the threat of an aroused town. It was a part of their rough and childish code. He had beaten the best of them and they would honor it.

"All right," he said. "Remember this. Mickey Dan was top dog in the Quinn's crew. He started the riot yesterday and he was ready to do it again this evening. It's always that way. In each gang of you there's a leader. If there's more trouble, I'm going to track down the man who started it. I'm going to whip him, and I'm going to throw him in jail. And if I have to go through every crew on the railroad, I will."

Again that mutter ran through them, and the sound of their shifting bodies was like a sighing of the wind. He saw that they were impressed. But there was still one thing left to do. He had put on a show for them and now he had to finish it.

With a deep grunt he reached down and hooked his hands into Mickey Dan's suspenders and started dragging him down the street to the jail.

CHAPTER SEVENTEEN

Scott never knew how he made it. Somehow he got the man to the cell-block behind the office and dumped him on the floor of the first cell. Then he leaned against the door and closed his eyes and let the sickness of the beating and the exhaustion take possession of him. He could fight it no longer, and he had no measure of the time he sagged there, breathing feebly, aching and throbbing. Finally he heard Mickey Dan groan softly.

He opened his eyes and saw the man trying to pull himself to a sitting position. He stumbled to him and helped pull him over against the wall.

"That was a helluva way to win a fight," Scott said.

"Fair and square," Mickey Dan said. "I never hesitated to kick somebody in the face, if I thought it was his weakness."

There was a rush of feet from outside and Penny hurried in. Shock widened her eyes as she saw them, and her first impulse took her toward Scott. He shook his head wanly at her. "Mickey Dan probably needs help worse than I do."

Mickey Dan groaned. "Help, is it? Hold him up, Penny, before he falls flat on his face."

She started once more toward Scott, then stopped again, looking back at Mickey Dan. "Oh, ye both need help, and I'm only one woman. Where c'n I start . . . where c'n I start?" She touched Scott hesitantly, tenderly. "Oh, the blood on ye. . . ." She turned and dropped to a knee beside Mickey Dan. "Is it broken ribs? Why don't ye lie down, ye blatherin' fool?"

The overwhelming reek of tobacco was wafted in to Scott and in a few moments Sean Quinn followed it. He stopped in the doorway, surveying them disgustedly.

"A fine, upstandin' pair o' men, brawlin' in the street like schoolboys, rootin' and crawlin' in the dirt like somebody's pigs." He scratched at his beard, looking at Scott. "I hoped t'see ye again, but never in sich hopeless disgrace."

Scott wiped caked blood from his jaw. Sick as he was, he felt glad to see the little section boss. "Talk to your bully boy about that," he said.

Quinn took a wallet from his pocket. "I understand you're marshal now. I suppose there'll be a fine."

"Not a fine, exactly. A week in jail or dock him two weeks' pay."

203

Sean's whole face squinted up. "I can't afford to be losin' him for seven whole days."

"Two weeks' pay?" Mickey Dan was aghast.

Quinn chuckled. "Keep that up and ye won't have nobody to fight with of an evenin'."

"The idea exactly," Scott told him. "You can pass it along to the other crews. It's what will happen with every man that starts a brannigan."

"Ye got us over a barrel," Quinn said. "Looks like y'r docked fer two weeks, Mickey, me boy."

"And he'll stay here till you're ready to go back," Scott said.

Quinn agreed, and they locked the door on the Irishman. Penny got a pail of water from the café next door and helped Scott wash the blood off his face and body. His shirt was ruined, and Penny took the Studebaker wagon to the realty office to get him a fresh one. When she had left, Quinn put a fatherly hand on Scott's shoulder.

"I had t'be stern in front o' me daughter, but they tell me that was the biggest brannigan since Mickey and me whipped four graders in Omaha. It's good t'see ye again, Scott. I hope y're marshal here when I come back f'r good."

Scott thought of the house up on the cliffs, and the sound of the trains coming through in the night. "I hope so, too, Sean," he said.

They smoked together while they waited for Penny. When she returned, Scott donned the shirt, put his coat back on, and rode in the wagon with them to the main street. The crowds moved restlessly through the night. There was shouted laughter and cursing and men calling to one another through the blackness, and the endless sound of tramping feet. Scott and Quinn dropped off the buggy by the T-Rail. Penny held the reins, looking down at Scott. Her face was but a dim blur and her voice was husky.

"I'll be back later with a pot of coffee," she said.

"This is no place for you," he said. "Take it to the jail. We'll drink it with Mickey Dan."

She nodded and drove off. Quinn went down to the Tie-Camp to watch over his brood and Scott stepped up to talk with Charlie Duncan at the door of the T-Rail.

"You took the vinegar out of 'em," the old stage-coacher said. "Been nice and quiet since."

"Anybody gets too drunk, stick their head in a water butt," Scott said. "I'll cruise now."

He checked his other deputies and found things in order. Leaving the Tie-Camp, he saw the long figure of Marshal Olvis, lounging in the door of the Ute Hotel, next door. He lifted a finger to his hat brim as he passed. Olvis nodded without smiling.

Past the man, Scott felt the marshal's poker-faced attention on his back, like a pressure between his shoulder blades, and he was remembering that meeting on the corner, Olvis and Bannack. What had been said? What had been told? Nothing. How could it be? If Bannack had exposed Scott, Olvis would have moved. Bannack wouldn't put himself in that kind of jeopardy, anyway. Yet that pressure remained between his shoulder blades all the way up the street.

Later on a man came from Duncan with word of trouble brewing in the T-Rail. Scott pushed into the crowded saloon and found Duncan with a group of men at the rear. A grader claimed one of Bobo Tanner's housemen had stacked the cards. The houseman denied it. Scott persuaded Tanner to refund the money the grader had lost and hustled him on to the Royal Flush.

The railroaders were beginning to leave by midnight. With the crowds thinning on the street, Scott saw the cut-under wagon standing in front of the office and risked a few minutes for coffee. Penny was there with the pot and four cups. He unlocked Mickey Dan's door and passed a cup to him. Scott and Penny were back in the outer office when Doc Gandy tramped through the door, dusty, stooped, rubbing bloodshot eyes. Scott grew tight with sudden tension. He forced himself to rise, to speak.

"Looks like you could use a cup of this."

"I could." Gandy lowered himself to a chair, sighing wearily. "Why can't they get sick where a buggy can go? My bones ain't fit for a ride like that."

Scott poured the coffee. "The man all right?"

"That bullet had been in there for months, festerin' and poisonin'. I don't know why he's alive. The arm should've come off. They wouldn't let me. Best I could do was probe it out and cut away some of the infection. If he lives, it'll be a miracle." He drank some of the coffee, squinting his eyes. "Thought I'd better tell you. The old man fitted the description the *Index* gave of this Yankee Walker. Rawboned, white-headed, crazy mean. Something wrong with his mind, Marshal. I took that woman, Jade, aside and told her what to expect, but it was wasted. She told them she wanted to ride back to town with me to get you. Only she didn't. She went instead to that cabin the railroad field man, Harvey Kane, has up on the Green. How well do you know those people, Scott?"

Scott saw Penny's eyes swing to his face, filled with a sudden darkness. Her lips parted. Scott spoke stiffly.

"That's a long story. I couldn't be of much help, anyway. I don't have any jurisdiction outside the city limits."

"You can still inform the government," Gandy told him. "They're lookin' for these Walkers. If you know these people, how come you told me that cock-and-bull story about their being called Fannin?"

"That's the name I know them by," Scott lied. "If I do go to Marshal Olvis, he'll want directions."

Gandy took out a pencil and drew a map on the back of an old envelope. Scott pocketed it, acutely conscious of Penny's attention on him. The doctor finished his coffee and took his leave. He still had his suspicions, or was at least confused, but he was too tired to want to pursue the matter further.

After he had gone, Penny said: "Jade. Is that the one?"

He walked to the door that Dr. Gandy had left open

and looked out into the night. "Yes," he said.

"We've been honest with each other, Scott?"

"As honest as I could be, Penny. She's gone from my life, but I still care about her. I've been hunting for something ever since the war. The good things. Sunshine, beauty, laughter. How can you put words to them? They exist. That's all you know. And when I saw you, I thought I'd found them again. All of you, Mickey Dan, the Quinn, this town . . . the end of a search."

She came to him and they embraced, kissing deeply. Then Penny looked up at him, something stricken in her eyes. "What are you going to do?"

"I'm not sure. Harvey Kane's up on the Green now. Jade's with him, according to Doc Gandy. He knows something. I have to talk to him. But I don't know how much good it'll do when it comes to helping my father. The man Yankee killed he thought worked for Bannack . . . and he did, but U.S. Marshal Olvis tells me now that the man was actually a government agent, working under cover. That changes things. If Yankee was justified in killing someone, it wasn't the man he did kill."

She stood, lips compressed, tears shimmering now on the surface of her eyes. She reached up and took hold of one of the buttons on his shirt. It was an impulsive, helpless little gesture. Her head bowed. "Scott," she murmured. "Oh, Scott. . . ."

He turned and led her back into the room. Picking up his coffee cup, he stared into it and finally tipped it up to finish what was left. It was only the dregs and it tasted black and bitter.

By two o'clock the town was almost empty of railroaders. The next day was Sunday, and Sean Quinn told Scott he would stay over at Mrs. Cassidy's with Penny, so Mickey Dan could sleep the night out at the jail. Scott dismissed his deputies after Sean left him at the T-Rail. Every joint in Scott's body ached from the battle and there was sand in his eyes and the need of sleep was close to pain. Yawning prodigiously, he started down toward the realty office. Approaching the Royal Flush, he saw the dim outlines of a figure leaning against the wall beneath the wooden awning. The man lit a smoke and light flared across Taw's battered cheek bones. Scott stopped beside him.

"You're not moving around enough, Taw."

The man grinned, looking at Scott out of half-shut eyes. "Bannack would like to talk."

Scott hesitated a moment, trying to decide what it could mean. Then he pulled his Colt.

"Let's go."

Taw looked down at the long, blue-black revolver. "Won't you ever trust me, Marshal?"

"Some men are fools," Scott said. "Some are heroes. I'm just an ordinary citizen, Taw, trying to keep the holes out of his hide."

It was the same side door leading off the alley into the same hall in the Royal Flush, the same room opening off the hall and the same smell of apricot brandy and the same maps on the wall. Only this time Garrett Collins was there, too.

He jumped out of a chair as soon as Scott entered, and fear gave a sucked-in look to his cheeks. "They told me you were here," he said.

Scott smiled reassuringly. "I am *now*." He looked at Kalispel standing, nervous and bright-eyed, by the window. He looked at Bannack, seated behind the desk. Cabinet was not in evidence.

"This time," Bannack said, "I'd appreciate it if we could shut the door."

Scott nodded at Taw, and the man closed the door with a gentle *click*. Bannack leaned back. The blandness was gone from his broad, freckled face. There were creases of weariness, of tension at the corners of his eyes, and his compressed lips held no humor. He brushed a hand tiredly across his forehead, stared down at the desk a moment, then looked up at Scott.

"All right," he said. "We're ready to bargain."

Unsure of his ground, Scott parried. "Marshal Olvis making you nervous?"

"Not only Olvis." Bannack leaned forward, locking his hands together on the desk. "You know we've got to get that lease before the railroad reaches here. Now it's been a good game and you've won. We're willing to settle."

"You're assuming we want to settle."

"What the hell!" Bannack said. "You didn't checkmate me just to keep this marshal's job. And Collins

210

isn't in on the deal just because he likes the way you part your hair."

Scott was beginning to see the man's reasoning now. In a way, it was the same way he'd have figured it, if he'd been in Bannack's boots. Bannack thought of Collins as a land shark, and to that breed of man money was a prime motive. On the surface, what else could Scott hope to gain from the game he'd played here? Even if he had evidence against Bannack, he'd still be laying himself as well as his family open to the murder charge by exposing him.

"All right," Scott said. "We'll talk business. We want a percentage."

The man's massive head came up angrily. "Are you crazy?"

"You didn't think a few thousand would buy us off, did you? A percentage, Bannack, and proof that what you've got here will pay us off."

Suspicion kindled in the man's eyes. "If you know about Cheyenne Parks, you know it'll pay off."

"For all we know you may have sold out Cheyenne Parks already. We're talking about the Palisades. You show us proof and we'll go on from there."

"What kind of proof?"

"The field notes that show what really is up there."

Taw made a disgusted sound. "You think we're fools enough to keep that around?"

It was Scott's last gamble. He had seen the careful way Bannack had covered himself in Laramie. Such a man would always leave a back door out.

"I think you would," Scott said. "If worse came to worse, you could cover yourself by turning up the original notes. I think you already have an explanation for the discrepancy. Who'd contradict it?"

"The field man," Bannack replied, sitting erect in his chair, staring at Scott. Kalispel began tapping his fingers against his leg in a nervous little tattoo. Then Bannack settled back with a heavy sigh.

Scott saw the defeat, the acquiescence in the slack lines about the man's mouth. With a sharp sense of triumph, he could not help glancing at the safe.

"Do you think we'd keep that kind of dynamite right here?" Bannack asked. "Harvey Kane still has the field notes."

Taw took a sharp breath. "You damned fool. . . ."

"Shut up," Bannack said. He rose, circling the desk, saying to Taw: "We can't afford to stall around any longer. Scott knows what he's getting into." He looked at Scott. "Before, we didn't know whether you were bluffing or not. We could afford to string along and wait for you to break under the pressure. But those field notes are the real thing. Once you see them, you're in it for good. We can't afford to have a man walking around knowing about them unless he's with us. Do you get what I mean?"

"Is Kane with you?" Scott asked.

"I believe he is," Bannack admitted, "but he's been stalling. He's been living in an old cabin up the Green while he's been running his lines around here. It's about two miles upriver, a half mile back into a timbered gorge. We can't leave in a bunch with Olvis in town. I don't know what's in his mind. Maybe he's working on a lead. Maybe he's just suspicious by nature. Either way, I think he's watching for something. So we'll have to leave separately. Just be sure you get out of town before dawn. We'll meet you at the cabin about an hour after sunrise. One way or another, we have to get those field notes."

"You were right in the beginning," Scott said. "I know what I'm getting into."

Bannack looked at Kalispel, at Taw.

Taw stirred uncomfortably. "All right," he said. "What the hell?"

Bannack nodded, spoke. "A deal?"

"A deal," Scott said.

Bannack gave Scott directions on how to find Kane's cabin, then he nodded at Taw. Taw opened the door. Scott nodded at Collins, and the realty man preceded him into the hall. They did not speak until they were in the dark alley. Then Collins let his breath out in a soft explosion.

"You were hopping around too fast for me, son. I never thought you'd make it."

"I didn't know where it was leading," Scott said. "But I don't think Bannack would let us in on those field notes unless we really had him against a wall."

"It may simply be bait to get us out of town," Collins said.

Scott had thought of that. With Olvis here, it would have been too dangerous for Bannack to try to get rid of Scott right in town. "We've got to take that chance," Scott said. "One way or the other, this looks like the break we've been playing for."

"How can we use it?" Collins asked.

"You go to Marshal Olvis. Tell him the whole thing. Tell him about Harvey Kane and the field notes. Get him up to that cabin."

Collins stopped at the alley end, touching his arm. "The *whole* thing?"

"Yes. It'll clear you. My identity is bound to come out anyway. This is our chance, Collins, and we've got to take it. Stand or fall, we've got to go whole hog."

"What about you?"

"I'll meet you at the cabin. I've got something to do first."

CHAPTER EIGHTEEN

Scott went a roundabout way to Holichek's livery. He was bone-weary but there was an urgency in him that would not let him stop now. He was thinking of Yankee, remembering his rages in Laramie, his obsessive hatred of Bannack. Yankee would know Bannack was in Green River now and Scott was afraid of his coming in and blowing the lid off everything before that meeting in the morning. He had to reach Yankee and stop him. Everything hung on the meeting with Bannack at Kane's cabin, the fates of all of them. He couldn't let one man's half-crazed need of vengeance ruin their only chance.

Scott let himself in the livery by the back door, saddling his horse quietly. The animal had fed well, had known a long rest, and was fidgety and eager for the trail. Scott left town by the back alleys, stopping half a dozen times to check behind him, but the town was black and silent, with no sign of Olvis in the streets.

Following Gandy's map, he rode seven miles upriver to a bend, found a lightning-struck cottonwood in a cove and a wash behind it that led into a deep cut. This opened out on a game trail that wound through broken hills matted with scrub oak. The trail branched within two miles, and the right fork led him to a clearing in which stood a log cabin. Green River had been a trappers' rendezvous in the old days and this was perhaps one of their places.

Age and weather had bled chinking from between the logs to pile in chalky heaps at the base of the walls. Through the cracks came yellow threads of light from within. Some fresh poles had been lashed to the decrepit corral and within the enclosure horses snorted and whinnied at Scott's approach. The light showing through the cracks blinked; otherwise, the clearing was shrouded in darkness. Scott pulled up. He heard the soft scrape of a door at the front of the cabin.

"Yankee?" he called. "Feather? It's Scott."

There was a space without sound or movement, then a shadowy figure emerged from the shack's interior. He rode toward it, trying to identify the shape. Feather's voice came to him.

"Scott, Scott. . . ."

The kid ran, stopping by his horse, reaching up to grab at him and pull at him. Scott dismounted, seeing Feather's face as a dim shape of hollows and planes in the darkness. Feather pounded him and hugged him and then pushed back, embarrassed by such a display, still hanging onto his arms.

"Scott, what in hell happened to you? I never thought we'd see you again. . . ."

Feather's voice died out, as though he had just become aware of their father, standing on their flank. Scott looked past Feather at Yankee's tall, dim shape. Yankee reached out and grasped his arm, stiff and inarticulate as always before strong emotion. Then in a brittle voice he said: "Let's go inside . . . Son."

Scott hitched his horse to the corral and walked between them to the cabin. Feather's grip on his arm grew tighter as they approached and a stiff silence had come to the boy. They stepped through the open door into a cramped room filled with the smell of decay. It took Scott a moment to register the whole scene, his eyes going to one of the sagging bunks ranged against the rear wall. Noah lay on it. He had come up on one elbow, like something out of a nightmare.

All the bulk of muscle had melted off him. The gaunt bones of his shoulders prodded at his filthy undershirt like massive knobs. His hair was a wild bramble, long as a woman's, and a three-inch beard covered his belligerent jaw and crept into the hollows of his cheeks like some parasitical growth. His eyes, sunk so deeply in their sockets that they seemed to be staring from a skull, were bloodshot and filmed with fever and pain.

Scott, notwithstanding what the doctor had told him, was not completely prepared for the sight, and shock held him speechless for a moment. Then compassion ran through him, pure and simple. All the old clashes, the obscure antagonisms, were driven out and he started for Noah in a simple impulse to do something for this man, his brother.

"Damn you," Noah said. "Why did you have to come back?"

It stopped Scott halfway to him.

Noah made a rattling sound in his throat and lay back. His mouth twitched uncontrollably at the corner and he stared fixedly and malevolently at Scott.

Yankee circled into Scott's vision. He looked almost as bad off as Noah. His face was ravaged. There were deep hollows at his temples and beneath his sharp cheek bones. The lines and seams lay like erosions in his flesh, and the muscles of his neck stood out like strings. He had a beard, too, like a gray-white fur on his gaunt jowls. His whole face emanated an aura of senility.

It was another shock to Scott. Yankee had always been a vital man to him, an embodiment of youthful stamina, violence, drive. Now for the first time Scott saw him in terms of age. Where time had failed, some inner corrosion had succeeded.

Yankee saw the look in Scott's eyes and made a husky sound. "What'd you expect? You'd look the

217

same way if you hadn't run out on us! Sitting down there fat and sassy under another name while we're living like animals. . . ."

"Run out?" Scott asked sharply. "I went to Rawlins Springs. A man named Rapp told me you'd only stayed there a day."

Yankee moved restlessly across the room. "Feather and me wanted to stay. Jade wouldn't let us."

"We had to get Noah to the doctor . . . ," Feather said. He moved to one side, looking at Scott intently. The boy showed the same signs of the terrible strain they'd all been under. He had lost weight, too, and the delicate bones of his face showed almost luminously through the sallow flesh. His pants and duck jacket were black with filth and grease and there were running sores around his neck, angry red and infected, where his collar had rubbed him raw. "Jade was right," he said. "I think Noah would've died if we hadn't got him to that first doctor. We thought he'd be all right for a time. Then it flared up again about a week ago. Doc Gandy said something about the bullet splintering against a bone."

Yankee was watching Scott fixedly. There was a little flame burning in his eyes, a crazy little flame. "So you came to Rawlins Springs?"

"I did." His tone was defensive, and he wondered why he should be on the defensive with them?

"And looked for us afterward?" Yankee pursued.

Scott started to speak, then he closed his mouth. How could he tell them, with Noah there, what had happened to him at Rawlins Springs? He had thought the choice Jade had made was concerned with him, but it hadn't been. Yet it had forged a decision in him.

Yankee's smile was like a grimace on his face. "I guess nobody could have cut our sign after Rawlins Springs. We were jumping around like hop toads." He circled the table again, working his hands together.

"Where's Jade now?" Scott asked.

"I could ask you the same thing," Yankee said gruffly. "She told us she was going back to town to fetch you up here. We let her go back with that sawbones. Ain't you seen her?"

"No, I haven't," Scott said.

"Well, it's no matter. She'd be of no help. You're here now. That's what counts. It just makes one more of us when we go after Bannack."

"That's what I came about," Scott said. "You've got to hold off."

Yankee wheeled on him. The flame was brighter in his eyes. "He *is* in Green River, then?"

"Pa!" Scott broke in on Yankee's shrilly rising voice. He took a step toward his father. "You've got to get this straight. I've got Bannack to a point where we can prove what he was doing in Laramie. . . ."

"We know what he was doing," Yankee said savagely. "He was riding with Quantrill again. Burning innocent people out of their homes. Turning them into hunted things, running like animals. What do we care what he was doing? It's past that now. He's the man we want."

"What good would that do? You'd just have another killing to your name. You'd be running the rest of your life."

Yankee's mouth was working savagely. "Maybe it's worth it . . . to see Bannack get what he deserves."

"So you want to drag all of us down with you, just so you can get your revenge." Scott glanced at Feather. "You want to make the kid pay and Noah and Jade . . . ?"

Yankee wheeled on him. "It happened to them, too. They were burned out, too. It was Noah's cabin. It was a year cut right out of Feather's life for nothing. . . ."

"Does he want to kill Bannack?"

Yankee wheeled on Feather. "Tell him," he said. "Tell him what any Walker with guts in his body would say."

Feather's mouth opened; his throat worked. Looking at Scott, he started to shake his head. Then he stopped and turned his back to them and walked to the wall.

Scott looked bitterly at his father. "Right now they only want the rest of us for complicity in Riordan's killing. Maybe that would mean five years. If you drag Feather and Noah into killing Bannack, you'll all hang. . . ."

"After what Bannack did?"

"The law doesn't know what he did. If you kill him now, all they'll know is you've added another murder to your list. There's another way. I'm trying to give it to you. I'm meeting with Bannack at dawn. There'll be evidence of how he's been juggling the surveys. A government marshal will be there. It's got to be this way. Bannack thinks I'm afraid to put myself in the hands of the law. But I'm through running. If we can prove what Bannack was doing, the whole thing will look different to a jury."

"How different?" Noah asked. He was still lying on his back, bandaged arm across his chest. His eyes had been fixed on Scott from the beginning, feverish, baleful.

"Riordan was a government man," Scott told them. "We thought he was working for Bannack. He pulled a gun. Yankee was crazy mad over the burning and lost his head. A jury'd see it different than cold-blooded murder. Instead of hanging, maybe it would be ten or fifteen years. . . ."

"So you want to hand your father over to the law," Yankee said. He circled the room once more, hands opening and closing. "You want to hand your whole family over to the law on a flimsy thing like that. I'd rather run the rest of my life. I'd rather live like this. Ten or fifteen years. How do you like that? I'd be seventy when I got out. I might as well be dead. . . ."

"Dad," Feather said, turning, "he's right. What else can we do?"

"Shut your mouth!" Yankee said. His voice filled the room like a roar and Feather's whole body jerked. Yankee wheeled on Scott. A little muscle was twitching at the corner of his mouth and that crazy light blazed high in his eyes. His voice held the same note Scott had heard back in Bannack's office that

221

day, trembling, choked. "I thought you'd come back to us. I thought you'd come to help us and stand by us and be with us when we paid back the man that did all this to us. And what do I get? A traitor. My own son, handing us over to the law like we were a bunch of common criminals."

"Yankee, you're twisting it. . . ."

"Twisting it, hell!" Yankee's voice grew soft and sly and mocking. "We decline your offer. You can go back and tell the marshal your little trick failed."

"I haven't even seen the marshal. It's not a trick. . . ."

"You can tell him I'm going to get Bannack." The slyness left Yankee and his voice began to rise again shrilly. "I'm not going to depend on laws that change everything around and let a man like Bannack go on killing and burning, and put the blame on his victims, on the law-abiding and God-fearing and the innocent that wanted nothing but a piece of land, a roof over their heads. . . ."

"Yankee. . . ."

"Get out, Scott!" Yankee's voice was near the breaking point and there was a fanatical shine to his face. "You aren't my son any more. I don't know you. Get out!"

Scott stared helplessly at Yankee. He knew he was through here now. The man's wild and unreasoning rage had defeated him completely. It was no use to speak any more. "All right," he said. He looked at Feather. "You don't want this any longer, do you?"

The boy started to answer.

Yankee spoke savagely. "Feather!"

The boy stopped, holding himself rigid. The look on his face was close to pain. He stood as if mesmerized, unable to take his eyes off Yankee's face. Scott wondered how this violent, rigid man could have such a hold on them. Had he been that subjugated by Yankee once?

Completely beaten by it, he turned and walked out. He moved around the corner of the house, and then stopped in the darkness, feeling sick with reaction to the emotional storm he'd gone through. He still couldn't believe what he'd seen in them. Noah, perhaps, was understandable, a mind sick with fever and all the pain. But Yankee. What explanation was there? Scott could understand momentary rage. He'd been mad enough himself to kill at times. But how could the need of revenge burn so long in a man, night and day, never letting up, driving him that way? Maybe Noah's wasn't the only sick mind. Maybe that was the only answer.

He heard them arguing inside, Yankee's shouts, Noah's husky answers. A scraping sound from the cabin made him wheel. He saw Noah's shape, silhouetted by the light behind the door. The man was leaning heavily against the logs, bandaged arm hugged against his chest. In his other hand was a six-shooter.

"I thought so," he said. His voice was guttural and wild. "You didn't come up here to save us. You've got Jade in town and now want to turn us all in to the law."

Yankee came out the door behind Noah, then

Feather. The kid spoke sharply. "Noah, you can't. . . ."

"Don't come near me," Noah said. "He ain't satisfied to turn on us. He's got to steal his brother's wife. All along it's all he wanted. My wife. . . ." The last words left him in a shrill and broken tide and he jerked the gun up. His head was turned so that the light reflected dimly in the feverish shine of his eyes.

Feather ran in front of him. "Noah," he said, "you're crazy. He's your brother. No matter what else, he's your brother. You can't shoot your own brother. . . ."

"Get away! I'll shoot anyway. I'd rather kill him than lose Jade to him. Why didn't she come back with him? I know why. Get out of the way!"

His voice rose to a shrill crescendo, and then a film dulled his eyes and he swayed forward, the gun sagging. He reached up with his wounded arm to grab at the wall. It kept him from falling, but his face contorted and he shouted with the pain it brought. As he tried to lift the gun again, his face still in a grimace, Feather jumped at him.

The kid threw his whole body against Noah's arm. If the gun had gone off, it would have killed Feather. But he caught Noah in that instant while he was still trying to recover and his plunging frame knocked the gun against Noah before he could fire. Feather tore the gun from his hand and jumped back. Noah slid down the wall and crumpled in a heap on the ground, Feather still holding the gun, looking blankly at his oldest brother, then he wheeled to Scott, face slack and shimmering with sweat.

"I'll go with you now."

"Feather," Yankee said.

Feather wouldn't look at his father. He kept his eyes fixed on Scott and he spoke in a jerky spasm. "I'll go with you," he said. "I can't stay any longer. They're crazy, Scott, they're both crazy."

Scott walked to Noah and went to his knees beside him. He was unconscious, breathing shallowly. Scott reached out to touch him and spoke in a dismal voice. "His arm's bleeding again. We'd better get him inside." He looked at Feather. "Can you stick it out a little longer, kid?"

The boy's wide eyes shifted to Noah. His shoulders sank; his head dropped. "I guess so," he said.

"I didn't have any right to ask you to leave," Scott said. "Noah needs you." He looked at Yankee. He tried to think of him as his father, but he couldn't. Yankee was just a man, a crazy, twisted man, standing there. What was in his mind now? Would he go after Bannack alone? If he did, he'd probably go into town. Bannack would already be on his way to the meeting. It was the only thing Scott had left. He couldn't even help them get Noah inside now. He couldn't even give Yankee that much time.

He unhitched his horse and stepped into the saddle. He looked down on them and he felt very far away, like a man asleep, looking at dream figures.

"I'll be back," he said.

CHAPTER NINETEEN

Scott pushed his split-ear through a night growing black as the moon died. He backtracked twice to make sure Yankee wasn't following, and then he reached the river and headed south along the bank at a gallop. All the way he was thinking about Jade. He had thought of her in such shifting terms since Laramie. In contrast to Penny, she now seemed a thing of darkness, of bitterness, of tragedy. Gone was the laughter they had known together before the war. He thought of her helplessness in what had happened in Laramie and since, her confusion, and in comparison to Penny's robust self-reliance Jade seemed weak and clinging. But, again, he had been overlooking what life for her had been since Laramie, the months of being hunted, living the life of an outlaw that she had done nothing to deserve. For her to stay with Yankee and Noah because of an old allegiance that would have been burned out of most people long ago—to stay with a half-crazed old man and a bitter husband she had come to hate, because she knew she was the only bit of sanity holding them together, to stay when she wanted to run more than anything in the world—was wrong, terribly wrong, to expect of her. If, instead of heading for Kane's place, she had returned to town with Dr. Gandy and come to his office, were she to have seen him with Penny, where would that have left her? Even if Kane had been the

226

man who had shot Noah, he wasn't really allied with Bannack, at least not any more. The projected dawn visit proved that. Yet, if Jade was with Kane, her life would be in as much jeopardy as Kane's. The one thing that would make it even worse, of course, would be if his father and brothers were to follow him.

Erosion had turned the cliffs above him into weird turrets and bastions that cast their eerie shadows across him in fluttering succession as he galloped the laboring horse up the gorge. It would spread out into badlands ahead, and from this he knew the cabin was near. The scrub timber reached out for him. It led through immense granite rocks, sprawled like giant, half-buried slugs across the ruddy earth. The iron shoes of his animal struck fire from the stony earth as he forced it into a last desperate run into the narrow meadow where the cabin was situated. Kane must have heard him coming, for the field man swung the door open and stepped out before Scott reached the cabin. Scott pulled his heaving, blowing animal up in a swinging turn that scattered rocks and sandstone. Kane held a rifle.

"I'm Scott Walker, town marshal of Green River."

"I know all about that. Jade's told me."

"Is she here?"

"Inside. Sleeping."

"You've got to get out," Scott told the man. "Both of you. Bannack and his men will be here at dawn. It's too complicated to explain now. He wants your field notes. He says you're in with him."

"He's wrong. I grew suspicious of him already back at Laramie. I reported what I felt was his dishonesty to the government. They put an investigator on it . . . to work undercover. Riordan. The man Yankee Walker shot to death."

"I know about Riordan now. Olvis, a U.S. marshal, told me all about it in town. I've asked him to meet me here. But if Bannack gets here first, there's going to be trouble and both you and Jade are in danger."

"There's you and me. Can't we hold them off until, as you say, the U.S. marshal gets here?"

"Christ, Kane, I still don't know what it's all about. Bannack thinks I do. But that was just a bluff."

"Come on inside. I'll show you."

Scott dismounted and let the reins of his exhausted horse trail on the ground.

"Try to be quiet," Kane warned him at the door. "We don't want to wake Jade. She's been through enough . . . especially after having to flee her husband and your father tonight."

"Doc Gandy told me," Scott said in a low voice, following Kane into the small, two-room cabin, "about Jade's coming here."

"Jade's in the bedroom," Kane said in a whisper.

There was a drafting table set against the near inside wall of the cabin. A kerosene lamp was on it, the flame turned low. Kane put down the rifle and went through some papers stacked on one side of the table. He selected a couple of sheets in a folder.

228

"Look at these, Walker. They're my field notes . . . the ones Bannack wants now. They're from Cheyenne Parks where all the trouble started."

Scott took the papers from Kane's hands and moved closer to the dim light to read. On the cover sheet was scrawled a name and date: *Harvey Kane, June and July, 1867.* Silently Scott leafed through the pages until he came to one that read:

Corner in a drain, course S.E., as corner could not be permanently est. in true position. Therefore point 25 links the line E. of true corner where we set post in mound as per inst. Deposited charred stake to section 66 and 67, T.4 N.R. 5E of this witness corner borings were indicated. They reveal seam of coal thirty chains wide following course N.N.E. as far as lines were run. . . .

It was all Scott could do to keep his face blank. Coal. Like somebody turning on a light. There was coal in Cheyenne Parks.

"I think there's also coal in the Palisades," Kane said, "only I didn't come across it at the time I did the survey. I think Bannack did. Riordan may have guessed what Bannack was doing in Laramie. But your father shot him before he could report. That's how I figure it. But maybe not. Riordan was fronting for Bannack, after all. Green River will just be repeating what happened in Cheyenne Parks."

"Does Olvis know this."

"He should. As soon as I found out, I reported it to the U.S. marshal's office."

"Why not the railroad?"

"They pay me, but, by my way of thinking, for the railroad to claim any coal deposit here amounts to just about the same thing Bannack tried to do in Cheyenne Parks. He works for the railroad, too, or have you forgotten? I made a mistake in taking off with that posse after you Walkers. I know that now. I've known it for some time. But Walker had shot Riordan. That's why I went after you. Jade's told me about Noah. She says he's going to die."

Scott ignored the man's confession. He knew now what had happened. When the field notes came into Bannack's hands, he would change the whole survey before putting it in his book, altering the lines so that Cheyenne Parks did not fall in the railroad's section, omitting any mention of coal and making Kalispel's claim to the Walker land secure. The railroad, believing the Palisades worthless, would allow it to be sold to Collins—and Bannack was doing the same thing here he had done before with Cheyenne Parks.

"You and Jade stay in here. Bannack's coming at dawn. He and his men will be here soon. I'll go out and try to stop them. With any luck, Olvis will be here, too. You keep these notes."

Kane was about to protest, then thought better of it, and nodded, taking back the field notes. Scott passed through the door and outside. The pale milk of dawn was seeping into the sky.

230

He tethered his horse firmly, and then sought higher ground on foot, eventually working his way through the brush along the ridge above the cabin. It did not take him too long to find the man. A faint curl of smoke betrayed him. Scott crawled closer and saw Kalispel, sitting on a deadfall that overlooked the river. A rifle was across his knees.

Scott knew he could not get close enough to strike without betraying himself. So he worked through the brush to within fifty feet of the man, pulled his gun, and stood up in plain sight.

"Kalispel."

The man jerked around, started to pull up his rifle. Then he checked the movement, staring at the gun in Scott's hands.

"Drop it," Scott said.

The man's lips began to work against his teeth. Pale eyes still fixed on Scott's revolver, he said viciously: "I thought so. I told Bannack. I thought so."

"Drop it."

The man still hesitated. Scott saw his body begin to tremble. Finally, however, the rifle slipped from his fingers. Scott walked up to him, the gun trained on his belly.

"Turn around."

The rage turned to fear. Sweat greased his bony forehead and a little muscle twitched across his cheek. It was a gun that gave his kind their power. Stripped of it, they looked pretty miserable.

"I'll get you for this, Scott, if I have to wait in hell

for you, I'll get you. . . ."

"Do you want it in the face?"

Kalispel hung on his toes for a moment, a man close to breaking. Then, body trembling, fists clenched, he turned. Scott had never hit anyone so cold-bloodedly before. But somehow he was drained of compassion for this man. He struck with the barrel of the gun, just behind the ear, and Kalispel fell without a sound.

He was about to return to his horse for a rope with which to tie the man when he heard someone tramping through the brush below.

"Kalispel?"

It was Taw's voice. Panic gripped Scott for a moment. Then he stooped and dragged Kalispel back into the thick underbrush, dropping the rifle beside the inert body. He turned and walked down the slope toward the sound of Taw's passage. The man appeared, toiling along the draw. He stopped at sight of Scott, scarred face blank with surprise. He let a husky breath flow from him, asking: "Seen Kalispel?"

"Farther downriver," Scott said. "Told me to come on in." He walked down to the man. "I hope you've got Cabinet watching, too."

"In town, keeping an eye on Olvis," Taw said. "Where's Collins?"

"We left town separately. I hitched my horse back a ways."

Taw looked around indecisively, the breath coming out of him like steam. Then he beat his hands together. "Kalispel will show him in. It's cold as hell out here."

232

Putting his hands into the pockets of his dusty coat, he tramped ahead of Scott, back along the draw. Bannack was waiting there, ahead.

"You weren't followed?" he asked.

Scott grinned wickedly. "You think I wanted to be?"

He was thinking of Kalispel. What if the man regained consciousness before Collins and Olvis arrived?

Taw coughed. "Damn," he said. "It's cold here."

"I'm surprised Yankee found the borings at Cheyenne Parks," Bannack said. "We had 'em covered so a surveyor would have missed 'em."

Scott lied. "We were pulling those rocks out. You couldn't fool an old coal miner like Yankee." He looked at Bannack. "But this seam runs way off the acre that would have been covered by your lease."

The man grinned. "The law of apex, my friend. If a miner controls the land where a vein surfaces, he can follow the vein as long as it remains continuous. All we needed was the spot where the vein apexed."

"You're going to mine it?"

"Mine it or sell out to the railroad. Either way it's worth a million."

"But if you sell, you'll be admitting the fraud."

"Why do you think we let Yankee or Collins get the land? We're covered by legitimate buyers. Our names never appear. Back in Laramie I wanted Gaelbreth Riordan to lease from Yankee. Riordan's death ruined that. Kalispel had to step in and do it. It doesn't matter now. Out here it's Ed Cabinet. He'll simply be cutting

233

ties when he comes across the coal. He'll set up a corporation to mine it, or sell. How can I be implicated?"

"The railroad will find it mighty funny that your field man didn't find the coal. They'll look into the survey."

"So Kane happened to run his lines wrong. Can I be blamed for a field man's mistake? If Kane doesn't come in with us this time, he'll be dead. What can a dead field man tell anybody? The worst I can do is forfeit my bond."

The simplicity of it was hard to grasp. It left Scott a little breathless to think how close Bannack had come to pulling it off, and he hadn't been stopped yet. Where was Collins? With some effort, Scott kept himself from glancing at the cabin, visible below them in the distance. Taw shifted restlessly, and Scott knew he had to say something. Before he could speak, the muffled sound of shots beat against them, and then someone was shouting. In an involuntary reaction, Taw wheeled, but no one was visible. Then Kalispel's running figure appeared, and they could understand his high-pitched shouting.

"Bannack, somebody's else is comin', and it ain't Collins. Bannack, somebody else is comin'. . . !"

Kalispel had a six-shooter in one hand, black smoke curling from its muzzle to smudge the pale air. Scott saw the man's face, as Kalispel caught sight of him, and he knew the moment had come, the moment Kalispel had wanted since their first meeting. This was the time that made the man a perverted god, this

234

instant of smashing violence that was the obsession of his life. All that was written in the man's taut and shining cheeks, in the insane glitter of his eyes, so that Scott was already drawing as Kalispel brought up his gun.

Kalispel was running and Scott was standing motionless, and it was this that saved Scott. Their guns made a deafening reverberation in the dawn. Kalispel's bullet slammed into a log six inches to Scott's left. Scott's bullet caught Kalispel in the chest, jerking his whole frame, driving the air from his body in a deep cough as he pitched forward onto his face.

Scott saw Taw begin to draw a gun and heard Bannack coming up behind him, but before either of them completed their reactions, the rest of it happened, too fast for Scott to follow. The heavy pound of horses shook the earth underfoot and Yankee and Noah galloped out of the dawn light. They saw the figures in the draw before them and opened fire.

Taw broke before the deafening fusillade and plunged toward the cover of brush up the side of the draw. A bullet drove Bannack hard against the wall of the draw. As if pinned there, he began firing at the riders. His first shot hit Noah's horse and the animal reared and Noah pitched off. His fourth shot kicked Yankee from the saddle.

Then the gun slipped from Bannack's fingers, and he hugged his bloody belly and slid down the wall of the draw. Through the haze of dust lifted by the plunging, rearing horses, Scott saw Noah crawling toward him across the ground. The man had picked up Yankee's gun and his face was slack and shimmering with sweat and as crazy as Kalispel's had been. He fired. The bullet struck the earth just past Scott's side like the blow of a hammer.

"Noah!" he shouted. "It's Scott!"

"You won't have her, Scott, you won't have her."

Understanding what it was now, Scott's first impulse was one of defense. He checked his gun halfway up. Not his brother, not his own brother.

"Noah, for God's sake . . . !"

A bullet struck Scott's hand. The shock made his whole body jerk, and he felt the gun leap from smashed fingers. With a shout of pain and helplessness he wheeled and dodged.

"Noah, it's Scott. Stop it!"

"She's mine, Scott, she's mine. . . ."

A bullet smashed not a foot from Scott. He ran to the other side of the draw. The pain began to eat at his hand like fire and he felt like a fool, a coward, crouching in this draw, hiding from a madman, his brother. He heard the scrape of the man's body, crawling closer, closer, the only sound out there.

"Noah . . . !"

A shot blotted out his voice. Another came across in front of him and buried itself in the dirt close to him. Then it was only the scraping sound again, the crawling sound. There was not a scrap of cover within the draw. He'd have to climb up to the brush into which Taw had disappeared or race down toward the cabin to get away. Only he couldn't do that. Kane and Jade were there. Scott stood rigidly in the draw, sweating, filled with an awesome helplessness, straining for the sound of that crawling, sliding body. He could not even hear it now. What was it, in a man, that he could kill his brother?

"Scott!" someone called. He stiffened, wounded hand hugged to his chest. But it wasn't Noah's voice. It came again. Garrett Collins's voice, from a distance. "Scott, you can come out now. I think it's over."

He moved slowly up the draw. Noah lay face down, a dozen yards ahead. The breath of life had left his body.

Farther up, toward the ridge, Yankee lay on his back, staring up at the sky with sightless eyes. Beyond him, Collins and Olvis were standing. Collins saw Scott's wound and hurried to him. When he saw the ugly tear in Scott's hand, he fumbled a handkerchief from a pocket, solicitous as a mother hen, and started dabbing at the viscid blood.

"Sorry we're late, son. Cabinet tried to stop us."

Scott sagged against the wall of the draw. "Taw got out through the timber."

"We'll pick him up, sooner or later," Marshal Olvis said. Poker-faced, he dropped to one knee beside Bannack, who still sat against the wall of the draw, hugging himself. Olvis pried an arm away, peeled the bloody coat back, pursed his lips judiciously. "Ain't a gut shot. Looks like you'll live a while."

Scott said: "Harvey Kane's in the cabin. His field

notes will prove what Bannack was doing."

Marshal Olvis nodded, standing up. "What Collins told me about the Riordan killing doesn't jibe with Bannack's version. Noah wounded Riordan to keep him from shooting you, and then your pa finished the job." He squinted down at Bannack. "If you'll verify that in court, we can't even hold Scott or Feather for complicity."

Bannack looked up at Scott. All the malice was gone from his eyes, the antagonism. They were dull with defeat. His voice came on a wheeze of pain. "Sure. What's the difference?"

Scott shook his head dully. The shock of those last violent moments still gripped him. He stared at Yankee and tried to summon some emotion, some proper grief for his dead father, and could feel nothing. Maybe it would come later. He was looking at a stranger. Maybe it would come later.

Then Feather rode across the plateau. Jade and Kane had left the cabin and were approaching up the draw. When Jade recognized Scott, she came to him at a run. Fear whitened her face as she saw the blood on him, and then she let out a sob of relief as he held out his hand, showing her that was the only wound. Kane had caught up with her, and she turned, coming into his arms and burying her face in his chest as he held her. Feather was off his horse, staring down at his dead kin.

"I couldn't stop them." His voice sounded dead, mechanical. "I don't know how Noah made it. They got away from me, must have picked up Jade's trail . . . or maybe yours. . . ." His voice trailed off, and he was still staring at Yankee with an emptiness in his eyes, a bitter emptiness, and Scott knew that he, too, was wondering why no feeling would come, no pain, no sense of loss.

Collins put a hand on Scott's shoulder. "We'll have to get a wagon for Bannack. We'll bring them all into town then. You go ahead. There's no sense staying around here any longer."

Scott gripped his arm in silent thanks and walked over to Feather. He put his good hand on the boy's shoulder, and turned him away from the sight of their dead father, their dead brother, the men who had been lost to them long ago. With Feather on one side and Jade and Kane on the other, Scott walked toward the cabin and his horse.

"I can stay in this town," he said to Collins in passing. "It's a good place. I've got friends here. Collins and a smith named Holichek and a girl named Penny. She'll understand. . . ." It was a strange thing to say, and it made him slow down and glance over his shoulder.

Collins was watching him, and he nodded, and a little smile came to his lips. "Yes, Scott," Collins said. "She'll understand."

It seemed to take a weight from Scott's shoulders. He looked at Jade's tear-stained face, at Kane beside her. He felt like saying something to Jade, but nothing came to him. Again she had made her decision. It

239

could be that Kane would be a better man for her than he had been, and certainly better than Noah. The light of a new day was now shining strongly against all their faces.

"Get your horse, Feather," he said, and continued walking down the draw toward the cabin. "We'll ride into town together."

Center Point Publishing
600 Brooks Road • PO Box 1
Thorndike ME 04986-0001 USA

(207) 568-3717

US & Canada:
1 800 929-9108